RIP-OFF RED, GIRL DETECTIVE

and

THE BURNING BOMBING OF AMERICA

RIP-OFF RED,

GIRL DETECTIVE

and

THE BURNING BOMBING

OF AMERICA:

The Destruction of the U.S.

𝕶𝖆𝖙𝖍𝖞 𝕬𝖈𝖐𝖊𝖗

Grove Press / New York

Published simultaneously in Canada
Printed in the United States of America

FIRST EDITION

Library of Congress Cataloging-in-Publication Data

Acker, Kathy, 1948–1997.
   Rip-off Red, girl detective and the burning bombing of America : the
destruction of the U.S. / Kathy Acker.—1st ed.
      p. cm.
   ISBN 0-8021-3920-5
   1. Women private investigators—New York (State)—New York—Fiction.
2. New York (N.Y.)—Fiction.   I. Title.
PS3551.C44 R57 2002
813'.54—dc21   2002029415

Design by Laura Hammond Hough

Grove Press
841 Broadway
New York, NY 10003

02 03 04 05 10 9 8 7 6 5 4 3 2 1

Rip-off Red, Girl Detective was probably written in 1973. It was Acker's first novel. She later described it as a "pornographic mystery."

The Burning Bombing of America was probably written a year earlier, in 1972, after Piere Guyotat's *Eden Eden Eden.* I would like to thank Susan Orlofsky, who had been given a copy of the manuscript by Acker shortly after it was written, and who unearthed it thirty years later.

Both novellas are published here for the first time.

—Amy Scholder, Editor

RIP-OFF RED,
GIRL DETECTIVE

Part One

1. April 20

I'm five foot three inches brown hair curling all over my face, bright green eyes, I'm 26 but my body's tough from dancing if you know what I mean—well I got bored doing a strip, well first, I got bored doing that Ph.D. shit and being frustrated professors' straight-A pet, especially being faithful to a husband who spent all his time in bed dealing out poker hands; I left school, descended to the more interesting depths and became a stripper, even that finally bored me, so I decided, on my 26th birthday, to become the toughest detective alive.

This is the story about how I have kept myself from being bored.

I was lying in bed with Peter; he had on his leather jacket and wrist bands; I woke up as the noon sun hit my face through the window; a cat started howling. I put my hands around his hips, I could see the thick whiteness and the dark hairs in the insides of my eyes; my nose burrowed in his neck, then inside his ear as far as I could get. He turned slightly toward me so I could caress him better, and moaned I had fallen for him first because he loved to be loved and showed it. Most men act cagey and think they shouldn't show any feelings. Peter rubbed his blond beard against my cheek, moved his body against mine. Our legs entwined; I felt his breath against my ear, then his lips on the skin of the ear, his tongue darted back and forth. Shivers ran through my spine, I felt his hand on my left breast squeeze slowly squeeze, my lower muscles started moving. With my teeth I pulled at the hairs on his chin, moved my mouth up to his lips slowly pressed my lips against his, moving back and forth until I felt his mouth open. For a long time we kissed I could feel his lower body pulse against mine, his muscles hardened, I let my hand drift down to where I knew he liked to be touched best he wasn't going to get it that early as his lips started to touch barely touch my nipple as if they were the wind and the shivers started rolling again up down my spine, I let my fingers pull gently at the soft hairs under Peter's cock; I ran my middle finger up and down the muscle behind his huge cock, at the warm wet creases between his legs and cock, just between not-feeling and his feeling tickled. His legs opened, his breathing became heavy fast; I let my other hand curve under his body; my finger caressed his asshole, not into it, but just enough of a caress so that he remembered all the millions of wonderful nerves curling inside and around his prostate gland. The muscles around my clit started tightening and loosening; my consciousness and the center of my body became my breasts then my stomach then the whole abdominal region—I could smell myself—then the region of beauty and fur between my legs. Peter's hand slipped from my back down to the inward curve above my ass in response I pressed my thighs against his, I felt his cock rise and fall against my opening thighs. His finger slipped between my buttocks into my asshole I moved my body faster, usually I like to be licked but this time I was too hot, I thought I would come from just the touch of his hands. I never liked anyone as much as this. The covers became all tangled dogs and cats started howling in the streets we moved faster faster; "let's cut the crap," I said, "and get down to business."

I rolled on my back I like to feel solid weight on me; Peter quickly moved on top of me. I like to feel cuddled: I pulled the covers over his back, let my hands rest on his back under the covers. I could feel his cock throbbing against me, I couldn't wait until he got in me and the real shivers start spasms crawling up down my body like electric eels inside my nerves until I start coming and coming and coming. Peter starts purring like a kitten rubbing against my damp skin and hair I open my legs his cock hardens inside then I feel him move deeper the pain stops he moves deeper as the rhythm starts as he starts moving back and forth still slowly I rise up I move into my clit into every micro-inch his cock touches I roll over a swan's neck into a quick orgasm a good beginning! He starts, as I come, to move fast quick higher up against my clit my hands scratch his back at the edge of pain I come again all feeling centers in my clit ah ahh AHH take a breath aahh I roll to a peak. Down.

Take a breath.

As I fall into dream, he starts again moving slowly, this time gently long strokes against my cunt, so that I barely feel him inside me, I start moving with him without disturbing my dreams I'm buying a dress I design dark green velvet fur a slit up my right leg which is as long as Peter's leg to my black cunt hair sparkles as brilliantly as diamonds, the dream changes I'm buying the most gorgeous dress in the world I fall into piles of velvet thick white Chinese satins. As I start coming again remember I'm fucking, I throw my thighs upwards press my abdomen, now open to thousands of sensations, against his, I feel his cock tremble inside me, is he going to stop? Keep going. Keep going. His strokes shorten he moves from side to side to delay my orgasm no I can't stand it I throw my body against his, more! More! He starts moving back and forth again like I like it it's happening it happens again again!

"Did you come?"

"Not yet."

"I can't tell when the fuck you come."

I'm too sensitive I can't stand to have his cock in my cunt against my cunt, I can't stop coming, I keep moving. Barely so I can feel his desire. We fall to the left; his arm moves under me; his middle finger slips into my ass: that's the center of my brain! That's where all my thoughts are located! We swing against each other deep into the freezing then fiery center of the earth around, now it's working, I want to come to, I want to get mine in I can feel his muscles move beyond his will, tense some then more, we're still moving in curves only faster, faster and harder; his finger leaves my asshole: rays of light shoot inside me from by ass to my belly button to my clit: the Holy Trinity O it's coming I don't give a shit anymore where he's at or what he's doing; my clit and my mind are one being light shoots through my body clit to legs! Clit to nape of the neck and outwards! Heat shoots through my body! Sound supersonic fluorescent waves.

I've had enough for the moment.

Peter still keeps moving; I watch a mosquito dash against the light bulb; finally I make the decision. "Listen sweetheart."

"What do you want now."

"We can't fuck all the time; we've got to do something more exciting."

"We could stop starving."

"I can write a book. I want to do something better than fuck."

"You dykes are all alike: best fucks around haw haw."

"Shut up creep."

"Anyway fucking's a bore."

"I'm going to change my name. You're my brother and you're going to have to go along with everything I do, be my secretary, and wait for me until I return from each assignment."

"Where are we going to go?"

"From now on you're Peter Peter and I'm Rip-off Red the famous detective. We're going to go East; in spite of the Mafia, the Jewish Mafia, and Mr. Nixon, we're going to get rich quick."

"On the road?"

"Listen. This is a dream. We're going to New York to rip off the money. Everyone in New York's an anarchist or a junky and many of the anarchists are junkies. We'll wander through the zoo; when the zookeepers are in the bathrooms, shooting up, we'll jump into the seal ponds with the seals. We'll nibble at their black velvet ears, with our secret hands rub their businessmen bellies; we'll fuck in front of the lions until we're howling more than they are. Listen. I'm going to go out this second down to Tijuana, rip myself off a black satin detective suit so I can set up business in New York as soon as possible: we'll rent a floor in a building on Madison Avenue in the Sixties, two rooms bare of furniture like a Japanese hara-kiri house; we'll have a sign on the door:

> *Mr./Mrs. Red, Detective*
> *Peter Peter, Detective*

We won't wear guns but carry junk needles; anyone who opposes us will receive an instant high. You have to protect me in all emergencies and tell me I'm wonderful. Listen."

"You're wonderful," confesses Peter Peter. "Where're we going to get all this money?"

"Money doesn't exist, of course. Don't worry about it; I don't. I just want everyone to love me. To love me and you."

This is Peter Peter's fairy tale as he falls asleep: Afternoon has begun. He's going to be a millionaire, eat snails and wine, fuck as much as he wants.

End of the dream.

Peter Peter puts his head on my shoulder, his hand over my still wet hairs. Am I interested? I put my head near his right nipple, he doesn't seem to mind. My lips barely touch his nipple; then, as his hand presses against me, against my cunt, as his hand slowly opens and closes, exerting gentle constant pressure, I quickly brush my tongue against his nipple as it hardens. I turn my head to the side; touching his nipple excites me too much; I return, my mouth becoming my eyes and hands; I don't know what's happening, I can tell I feel strongly Peter moans, presses his lips hard against mine. I kiss his lips, this time move straight down to his white stomach; his flesh is firm and thick like a child's. Sexy as a child's. I curl my tongue into his belly button until the tip of his cock aches. Meanwhile my hands roughly massage his cock and balls squeeze pull, the more he pulsates, the harder I squeeze. I bite his inner thighs, pull with my mouth at the hairs around his balls; I roll his balls in my mouth; I run my tongue into his asshole and around toward his cock, do everything but touch his cock in order to drive him as insane as possible. I keep this up for hours: he moans; the moaning turns into harsh sighs. Suddenly I reach for his cock let my mouth slip over his cock until the tip of his cock is in my throat. I let my tongue alternately press at the undertip of his cock right at the edge of the hole then curl arabesques up and down the length of his gorgeous plunger. Quickly I spit into my hand, run my hand around his cock, corkscrew; in an opposite motion, twist my throat around and around. I play with rhythms: I start light and slow, go faster with heavy pressure and emphasis on the pressing tongue. As Peter moves faster I reach a low peak, then start again, slow, deliberate; I let him, rest, and slowly again get into moving with motion of my mouth and hands. I move my mouth and hands more this time, accentuate the corkscrew motion; we work together; I move faster, take more cock into my throat. No, I've lost him. I don't stop, but move more slowly. We meet; now I've lost consciousness; I'm a machine of throat, mouth, tongue, hand symmetries and pressures; my body pulsates in sympathy.

I no longer know if I'm doing a good job. This lasts forever; time intercedes, I can feel his cock expand; I push my tongue, my throat grasp; I become a gymnast, a snake; Peter moans; his whole body moves now his hands rest on my head I start sucking use my tongue more his cock grows enormous I can't his hands press my head down I can feel two muscles which run up the sides of his cock wriggle, the liquid rushes into my mouth I press my lips against him in rhythm with his coming, now. I lift my head up for air, quick swallow, then gather him in again was it good? Now I'm resting against his shoulders. Below my outer skin there's a layer of shining warmth; I savor my horniness, keep it till it increases impossibly.

2. April 28

We borrow money from Peter Peter's father, I'd love to fuck the whole family, and go to New York. I'm a tough dame.

On the plane, the mystery begins.

Peter Peter and I sit next to the window; we throw coins, Peter Peter wins the seat next to the window.

"You're an old shit-ass."

"I'll sleep with you any day. No, I'm too scared."

We drink two martinis, then I down a beer and two glasses of champagne. New York champagne, but these days there's a depression. I seem to be weightless; no, it's just the atmosphere inside the airplane. My body floats in waves, an endless air ocean. That's it, I'm as drunk as an Irishman; I'm both inside the airplane and outside, a true beautiful angel sailing among white elephants and kangaroos. What's this? The swirling area travels down to my stomach, around my half-asleep sweet ass, to my cunt; muscles move in and out between my legs, I try pressing my legs together, rub my lower ass against the seat. No one seems to be looking. There's a woman sitting next to me, on the aisle seat, mmm she's beautiful, well she's asleep. Is she pretending? I pull my coat over my legs to my waist; I've become a cripple. I slide my hand under the coat, under my black velvet pants, I'm pretending to read (I know how); I press the bottom end of the book against my clit, right below the bone, that helps a little, I move O just slightly! Back and forth, I can't be too obvious. The secrecy I usually hate makes my horniness build, the body of a woman next to me and completely untouchable, that's right, hands off! the whole public scene makes my nerves soar, white frenzy, in response to my frustration. Like a fox, a true detective, I sneak my hand under my pants, at least I'm not wearing underpants today, there's not enough freedom. I unsnap my blue jeans. No, no one's looking; they're all as drunk as I am, even drunker and hornier, and they're not going to do anything about it, they must have great dreams, I'll solve all their problems mmm. Peter Peter's head falls against my shoulder; I put my arm around him, kiss him on his soft neck, he's become a snoring bear. Meanwhile my hand, no longer part of my body, my fingers slowly caress the flesh above my hairs and between my legs. I want to play with my desires, I want to gain control of them so I can bring myself higher and higher to the most incredible climax possible. The plane disappears, the seat on which I'm sitting falls out from under me; I'm suspended in space by strings of diamonds the paws of cats rub against my ears. As my long fingers enter the mysterious hairs, the tight silk curls which cover my cunt, I rub the skin below my hairs quickly, then with the middle fingers press up and down above my clit, taunt the clit. I force myself to strain toward the orgasm, for my cunt to imagine the orgasm. My other hand, above the black coat, presses down on my womb; I concentrate on that mild delight, try to forget the more potent delight my fingers are giving me. My nipples swell, I can feel each tender pore; in the back of my eyes, I have a soft breast in my mouth, as my tongue plays with the nipple, it becomes harder harder. No, none of that; I begin playing the usual game with myself: my fingers belong to me and my cunt doesn't. I concentrate on how the flesh of my fingers feel as they caress a strange clit and deny the heavy pleasure my clit is showing. One finger, now, presses up and down up down above the clit, now just on the clit, not too hard yet, not too fast, just so the rhythm and pressure of the finger is a bit slower than the feelingless rhythm of my desire. Somewhere deep I still remember those sensations between my legs; I can't concentrate completely on just the feelings in the skins of my finger. Try harder. I disregard the strength of the approaching orgasm, I'm not scared because I'm not dwelling on the orgasm. No, I've lost myself: I'm not interesting enough to myself. In a book I'm a middle-aged housewife and I'm sick of fucking my husband. We've been happily and monogamously married for a hundred years. It's the midafternoon; my husband's away at work, we live in the suburbs. The doorbell rings. It's only the grocery boy.

"Just put the groceries down there." I look again; he's slight, dark-haired, he'd be sleazy if he wasn't sooo, so what? "What's your name?"

He trembles, looks strangely at me. "Why don't you come sit beside me?" I pat a space next to me, well, practically on top of me. He sits down, not so close, he's just a kid.

"Do you do this all the time?"

"I . . . I." He shivers. I take his hand, put it around me, on my violet breast, our lips meet. I let my hand fall to his cock, caress it.

Now my desire soars; my finger can't move fast enough, deep enough as I start to fly. Wait, slow down, control the waves so they last longer, roll deeper. I hold back, let myself rise. I lose myself, no, I have to start my finger presses again, rhythmically, forseeably, now. Now. Now. Now. I let the hard burning rise, my clit swells to unbearable proportions, suddenly I feel fur silk on my cheek a strange animal in my hair, I don't care what the hell's happening. I'm in a brothel and a thousand thick Arabs are seducing me. The muscles of my upper legs tense, my legs rise slightly upward from my calves. The legs and buttocks part from each other; the wave rises, down slightly, by will I make my finger move faster, the stranger pulls at my hair with thin fur fingers. I start orgasming stronger; I force by iron will my finger to move more rapidly, more crazily than possible; finally I begin to rise, I rise even farther, suddenly I move vertically: there: the queen. Before I know I've reached it, I've forgotten everything, two huge hands grasp my head and turn me toward another head. I look into huge blue eyes, I move my mouth toward the skin near the nose, then toward the mouth and we start to kiss.

I feel soft lips under mine, softer than Peter Peter's, they feel so soft I want to press into them again and again. I do, I'm sinking, my face is sinking into a thick quilt, through the tiny space among the fold of the cotton I let my tongue drift into this strange mouth. I don't want to stop, I don't even want to stay still, I might get scared at what's happening, I'd have to find out who I'm kissing. Our tongues touch, lightly, then mingle, saliva swirls around, I feel my spine disintegrate and my arms fall around this thin back. For hours we kiss inside each other's mouths stroke identical heads of curling hairs; my hands press under the ears.

Now desire doesn't center in my clit but turns around my body, my nerves swirl until my whole body shivers and trembles to touch this stranger in every way and everywhere. My mouth becomes even softer, thicker; my arms curve in toward the chest. My hands pass over her heavy breasts, to their bottom, low heavy soft breasts under a light sweater; I lay my palms over her nipples press gently, do you like that? Her wire tongue darts over my ear, she nibbles at the lobe of my ear so I'm slightly excited; suddenly her tongue pierces my ear ice-cold. I shiver; she blows into my ear and sends frantic nerve waves throughout my body how can I kiss her breast is everyone staring at us?

"Come to the bathroom."

"We have to be cautious," I whisper back, secretly. "You go first; when no one's looking, I'll follow."

She leaves me. What do I feel? What am I thinking? Do I feel anything? Five minutes pass by; I follow her. We squeeze into the tiny bathroom and start giggling. There's no room to move a hand, much less a tongue. I look at her, suddenly frightened and confused: do I dare touch her, could she possibly want me to touch her? I can feel myself blush, no, she's taller than me, prettier rather than beautiful, curly yellow red brown hair, a nose that seems to wink.

"Do everything I say."

I'll follow her implicitly; she can do anything to me except leave me. She takes my hand; with my fingers she strokes her eyelids, the skin directly below her hair, then her cheeks. I follow her, tell her I love her, I want to be her, we're beginning, now we're beginning. Are you still scared? She lifts my hand, it grows lighter, places it under her sweater; she strokes her breast with me, I'm her animal, I learn to stroke her breast. We're twins; breast against breast somehow.

"Can I suck your breast?"

The nipple burns my tongue; I can feel the child suction begin in my mouth. I pass my tongue slowly over the nipple; her nipples are large. Her hands rub my neck and shoulders so that I have to move even closer to her. We murmur; I murmur; I begin to suck again on her nipple, then on the other one as that one hardens, as her whole body tenses. I can't go through with this. I don't know how to give her pleasure. As I suck, her thighs thrust forward against my strained stomach and chest, she reaches downward her hand to my cunt; "I can't," "What do you want?" I'm scared. I let my hand fall against her cunt; she envelops me. "Kiss again," we kiss again. "Are you O.K?" I remember: I'm in school, we're two children making love, we rub noses and bellies. I sit on her lap on the tiny toilet: I can feel her desire, I can feel mine I put my hand on her pulsating cunt, undo her pants and touch her, she moves harder. I press one inch below her hair and lower, at first try not to press her clit lest I irritate her. She moves against. Each time she begins to move faster, I move my hand faster;

finally with thumb and second finger I touch her clit. Lightly, I press it systematically she moans into my ear I press the palm of my hand into her cunt bones I caress her clit I adore her clit I moan faster all I want her to do is come. Her fingers clench the back of my neck; I can feel her sweat. As she begins to move beyond her will, I thrust three fingers up her cunt, I rub her clit hard, fast insane motion, she peaks I think, I kiss her neck, she peaks again. I keep my hand on her cunt, pressing, until she calms down. Her head lies in my arms, I hold her, as proud as if I just had a kid.

She lifts me until I'm standing; I feel her hands rub against each of my sides. Her long fingers press into the fronts of my legs into my stomach. I remember her coming I pulse I want her to help me. She plays with me; I look down and see her face. Something touches my cunt. "Lower," our eyes meet, "that's too much. Lower." I feel her tongue touch the skins just below my clit; her tongue moves back and forth slowly. My hands rest in her hair, pull and scratch as she moves into me further and further. Her tongue rises, O, clicks against me I'm hot all over I can't concentrate "concentrate." As I begin to come, her tongue runs into my uterus, no, a man's fucking me, a soft hard cock's inside me, softer more delicious than a cock; my muscles fall open, I'm open to anything, I want my rising to start. The cock touches every inch of my vagina, every hidden flaming nerve soothes, each time she touches me I start coming. She rushes against me; her whole body throbs, I want her now I forget her I know only the soft pounding soft irritating of my clit, I want it there I go a little higher; there; each touch is another step. Every inch of my flesh is throbbing: shorter, quicker there I come in my ass there in my cunt, her whole mouth takes hold of me, I'm completely safe I come.

This isn't typical of a hard-boiled detective, a detective who chooses intellectual pursuits over emotional ones. I have no right to be scared. Well, I'm a female detective; I don't pay attention to that shit about intellectual versus emotional. I decide she's my sister.

We put on clothes.

"I'll leave first."

I watch her leave. I look at myself in the mirror; five minutes later leave the bathroom. As I return to my seat, she looks at me and brushes my cheek gently with her hand.

"What's your name?"

"Rip-off Red."

"Mine's Spitz. I've always wanted to be like you; you're not as scared as I am. I don't have any profession; I'm scared I'm useless."

"I'm a detective."

"You're a detective, a real detective, can I . . ."

"I was trained in the Sherlock Marlowe School for Private Eyes: I just got my degree this June. I'm going to New York because it's the most evil city in the world and it's my home. Frankly I like decadence."

"Would you, O I don't know if I can ask you; I don't even know if I can trust you." She bursts into tears on my shoulder; I don't know what to do.

"Listen. Peter Peter here's my partner." Peter Peter moans in a sympathetic drunken stupor, "so the two of us, Peter Peter and I, can help you; we're really good."

"It's my father . . ."

"I'm not too fond of fathers myself but I can . . ."

"My father's wonderful, he was wonderful, O I don't know what's happened to him, he just, he just left."

"Do you want me to find him?" I say in a low hushed voice.

"He hasn't disappeared; he just disappears at 10:00 P.M. every night, for three or four hours. He won't tell me where he's been, and well mother's also upset; we all don't understand it.

Strange checks appear on his bank register which are in his hand-writing which he says he doesn't remember writing out. He says he doesn't remember what happens in the hours every night he's gone from the house."

"I'll take it on," I say, "one hundred dollars a day plus expenses."

"I love you."

"I love you too."

I slip my hand under the coat, and caress her belly button. As I touch her cunt lightly, she smiles and kisses my nose. I continue pressing down, play with her; we move closer together. This is my and Peter Peter's first job; we have to be careful and not fuck up. If we do a good job this time, we could be on our way. I'm not sure if I know New York well enough.

"My mother says all our money's disappearing she doesn't know where."

"How old are you?"

"24."

"I'm 26."

"My father's a jeweler: he owns a huge diamond industry in South Africa and is a special envoy at the U.N."

"You'll have to give me all the names and addresses of the people involved. What's your name?"

"Sally Spitz."

"Will you sleep with me or with me and Peter Peter in New York?"

We smile. I can tell this job's going to be wonderful. A cinch.

Peter Peter wakes up and asks me where we are. I plan to meet Spitz the next day at her parents' house on East 57th Street.

3. April 28, April 29

The first vision of New York

"Here we are in New York; we better stop acting like hicks," I pronounce. Peter Peter and I stand in the airport terminal, looking around. Peter Peter's looking for a bar.

"I want some snails, and a decent wine," he moans. Actually New York looks like San Diego, at least so far, only there are fewer cops—airport ones and regular ones.

I'm thinking hard. "If we want to appear like New Yorkers, we'd better start looking like junkies. We'll never make the rich set." We pull up the lapels of our jackets, start slinking toward the bathrooms.

"Which way's the baggage room?" Peter Peter's going to wait for the snails until we get into the actual mysterious city.

Somehow we find the luggage room, in spite of our inability to read; through the fogs and clouds, we search for our suitcases. Suddenly I see Spitz ahead of me, a brown leather suitcase in her black-gloved hand. As I start to walk toward her, a guy approaches her. He looks like he's part Spanish, part Arabic, a moustache sweeps over his mouth, muscles step out of his skin. He's six feet two inches, weighs about 180 pounds. "Better not mess around," I think wisely. They talk to each other, then turn, and leave the room. I don't know who Spitz is, how trustworthy she is.

"Stop mourning," replies Peter Peter. "The whole world lies

at our feet. We still have two hundred dollars; let's blow it on sex as fast as possible. You'll see your true love tomorrow."

"You're my true love," and we navigate ourselves into the wild jungles of New York.

I wake up in a strange room. A man walks past me, sticks a knife into me. I get up I don't understand what's happening. I walk into the crevice between two buildings. A man walks past me; as he passes the crevice, his arms swing out to the side and he slips a knife into my body. I move sideways, race to a stairway, hide under the ice-cold steps. Thin drops of water fall on my neck. The man crouches down, comes under the steps. Our white eyes stare at each other. I'm in a cafeteria; a man approaches me; orders me to lie down flat, back on the table and take off my pants. "Everyone will stare at me."

"Do as I say."

The table's cold, slimy beneath my back. It begins to move.

"How little is necessary to make you come?" he asks. He leans down over me, presses his mouth against my breast, kneads the breast. As his tongue starts to flicker against the nipple, the nipple hardens. He begins to suck in my breast; I caress his head and damp ears. His wool jacket itches me; the itching excites me. "Let me do it to you."

I quickly take off his jacket and shirt, lightly run my tongue over his nipple. My body pulses in response. My lips close in on his nipple. I feel his nipple lengthen harden. I let my hand fall below, on his cock. Alternately my tongue flickers across his nipple and my mouth moves will-lessly, sucking as if I were a child. I am. As I suck harder, the muscles around my clit throb; a layer of heat builds up in my clit, spreads through my body. The heat grows, spreads three times, after which I shudder.

I have to get out of bed and see Spitz. Peter Peter looks at me, concerned. "Were you having a nightmare?"

"I'm scared. There's a man in the bathroom; go look."

Peter Peter walks past the bathroom. "It's only a blue robe. Calm down; we're in New York; everything's perfect."

"Do something to calm me down."

Peter Peter looks at me. Now he's the king. "Listen darling. Don't have nightmares." He puts his hand on my cunt and starts rubbing. "When I was thirteen, in Germany, I used to have nightmares regularly, especially about the bars I used to haunt so I could hear jazz. One nightmare which was both extremely horrible and extremely pleasurable would occur again and again. I was lying on a bed in a black room; the room or the space in the room became a huge ocean in which dinosaurs and green lizards leaped about. As long as I was touching my bed, I was safe. A woman came to my bed. She had a slender manlike body. She told me she was my father, that she didn't want to cause me pain in any way. I didn't understand what she was talking about. She lay outside, on the covers of the bed, body leaning against my body, and started to whisper words to me I couldn't hear or couldn't understand. Her right hand held up my head; her left hand rested on my waist. 'Would you like to kiss me?' I reach up and place my lips on her mouth; after a while I feel her body move as if something was twitching her. I place my hand on my cock which is surprisingly hard. This is my cunt. If I touch my cunt long enough, I'll become pregnant. 'Does this hurt you?' Fingernails scratch at my lower back, then at my legs. I say nothing. She begins to scratch me hard and pulls my head against her breast. I slowly begin to dissolve. Small yellow crabs start walking toward me, then two large orange crabs advance, a whole flock of crabs, all sizes, their claws clank open and closed.

"I wake up screaming. Mommy. Mommy. That night my parents were giving a small elegant party; at that time my father was a United States Consul. My mother detested leaving her guests to help me.

"A tall woman entered the room. I drew back frightened. 'Are you all right, Peter Peter,' she murmured, 'it's only Shyshy.' Shyshy was my nurse, a young girl from Munich, who had lived with us since I had been six. European nurses, you know, have strange but effective ways of calming children. I was so frightened and so confused by wanting my mommy, and wanting and not wanting this girl that I started to cry. Shyshy came over to me and put her arms around me. 'I'm better than your mommy; I'm younger than her so we can talk more openly.' I immediately unbutton a light blue lace blouse she's wearing, sort of like a night robe, and, as if it were an animal, stroke her breast. She smiles and puts her two hands on my ass, lifts me on to her lap, she's sitting Indian-style on my bed, so that my legs possess her thighs and our arms lie around each other's waists. Now I realize that she must have been slightly drunk, though at that time I was too curious and excited to question her sudden sexual interest in me."

I cuddle closer to Peter Peter, unzip his pants, and put his cock in my mouth. In his usual gentle way, he starts to stroke my head.

"We kept looking at each other and smiling; our faces slowly approached each other. As we again began to kiss, she took my right hand and placed it under her skirt on the silky cloth which covered her hair. I watch her body begin to move. I feel my own body turn into water, that's how it felt; I can't help myself anymore. She takes hold of my face, holds my face still, kisses me, her tongue delves deep into my inner regions. I can remember trembling. I remember her taking my clothes off quickly and softly; then still as she kisses me, she removes her lace blouse and a small wraparound skirt. Excitement races up down my body; the emotion's too heavy. A thin nerve or muscle from my navel to the tip of my prick tightens grows longer. She breaks away from me, takes off white lace underpants. My whole body trembles hard. I'm possessed. In some way I'm in control but I have no idea how. The muscle from my navel begins to pound harder; blood inflames my face and hands. My nerves are dead, they're too alive. I want to see her and I can't. She takes hold of my face, draws it over her body, in her cunt and out, as if her cunt's equal to the rest of her body; she takes my hands and makes them touch every part of her body. When I'm dying. I'm shaking into tiny pieces, I'm almost vomiting she draws my head again to her breasts. I can feel the lower part of her body tremble as much as mine. Suddenly something happens, as if I've been hit over the head; my cock's the only part of me left, growing beyond any masturbatory state, and I seem to faint."

Peter Peter stops talking. As I wonder what's happening, he clenches his hands around my head, pushes his cock into my throat. A muscle in his cock ripples; boiling liquid rushes into my throat.

So much for nightmares.

It's 3:00 in the afternoon. I put on my black velvet detective suit, black Indian silk around my neck, two pairs of silver earrings in my double-pierced ears, and walk over to the door. Spitz is living with her parents: First Avenue and 57th Street where Marilyn Monroe and Arthur Miller used to reside. Hot shit.

"Be careful," warns Peter Peter, "and remember your karate. This could be a dangerous assignment."

"What'll you do while I'm gone?"

"I'll sit here masturbating ha ha." Peter Peter's gentle warm and brilliant. A perfect partner. I walk quickly out into the strange New York streets.

Huge chunks of garbage burn my eyes. Finally I stop crying, regain my sight. I still can't breathe. Well, it's more important to see than to breathe. I walk up to a huge man who's wearing a black suit with a newspaper under his arm.

"Excuse me sir, could you tell me how to get to . . ." He stares at me, and walks away. Does he think I'm after his ass? I try again, walk up to an old lady.

"Excuse me, could you tell me how I could . . ."

"I'm sorry," she interrupts me. "I never give money to strangers."

I'm freaked. This whole town's freaked. I see a long-haired guy, no; I walk up to a cop. To cop, "Hey, how can I get to 57th Street and First?" He motions to a bus stop a block away.

O.K. I'm on the bus, have a few minutes rest until I get to my assignment. Everyone looks like they're on the nod. Across from me, a black guy looks at me, unzips his pants and shows me what he's got. No one reacts and he's bigger than me.

Now I'm walking down 57th Street: a young woman passes me and throws an orange at me. "You're so sweet and dainty now," she screams at me, "but you're like all the other people. You lie and hide your real feelings; you're going to have to whore and murder like the rest of us." I don't pay any attention to her; I'm a real New Yorker.

It's Second Avenue and 57th Street. I see a crowd down the street collect at the southeast corner. Another stupid murder. I stroll down the street slowly; I'm in no hurry. Thousands of cop cars race past me as if they're on speed. I pass by three apartment houses, a delicatessen whose windows display rattlesnake soup in cans, kangaroo's tail soup, chocolate-covered ants, chocolate-covered bees, turtle soup with sherry, finnan haddie, smoked oysters and smoked clams, sharks' fins, birds' nests, and other assorted goodies. Next door is a bar with beer kegs for stools. The real Wild West. I'm on the corner. The crowd across the street has grown to immense proportions, probably the bored rich and pickpockets. I debate whether I should go in for pickpocketing, decide not to, I'm on a detective assignment and have to keep respectable.

Let's see where I am. I take out a silver notebook. Spitz lives with her parents at 410 East 57th. I cross the street, wade through the crowd, trying to get to my building. "Who's been killed?"

"Some lady," a child answers. "She's awfully pretty."

Suspicion thunders at me. I barge through the crowd to the ropes. Two men are carrying a stretcher away; a white sheet covers a figure.

"Who's been killed?" I ask the nearest cop.

"None of your business; stay back if you know what's good for you."

I take out my detective credentials. "Who's been killed you sonofabitch?"

"Dame by the name of Sally Spitz according to the papers in her wallet."

When I come to, I run toward the ambulance. The cop holds me back. I'm never going to kiss anyone again. From now on my life's devoted to the logical inductive and deductive search for all criminals. I swear to dedicate my life to solving the mystery of Spitz's father, to avenging Spitz, and to avenging my murdered love for Spitz. I'll only make love with Peter Peter.

I have to find out how Spitz was murdered.

"Fifteen minutes ago, a bullet from a .38 special; no one saw anything. We're still searching for a witness." The cop's sick of me, and starts to walk away. I press a five dollar bill in his hand.

"Know anything about her father?"

People in the crowd are staring at me. Didn't they ever see a detective before?

"Don't have the faintest idea who he is, probably some hotshot if he lives around here." Flatfoot pockets the fiver and walks away.

O.K. Was Spitz killed because of her father. Because she had asked me to investigate her father's nightly disappearing and amnesia? For some other reason. Does anyone know she had hired me to investigate her father?

I'll have to meet her father and her whole family, but not today. I'll say I'm a friend of Spitz's.

Suddenly I feel very tired. I don't like New York at all. I turn around and start to walk slowly home.

As I'm walking past a brown brick building on 55th Street between Second and Third, just as the sun is going down, I hear footsteps behind me and note the lengthening of my shadow. I turn my head. I think I see a man; I feel pain; I slump to the concrete.

4. April 30

I move as fast as possible

"What happened to me?"

"I don't know." Peter Peter gently lifts my head onto some pillows. "Why don't you tell me."

"My head's killing me. Why didn't you just leave me all shattered where I was. Fuck this detective business."

"Some old biddy found you on the street and started screaming. God knows why with all the drunks and beaten-up people lying around on these streets. The cops found your address and brought you here after getting someone to plaster a bandage on your head. They told me this was our welcome to New York. That's all I know."

A great light flashes over me. I remember everything. This detective business is terrific. Then I remember Spitz's death.

"Spitz is dead," I sob.

"What the hell are you talking about?" Peter Peter yanks up my hair. Building rods made of stars clank together. I scream.

"Uh, sorry. Don't cry, baby."

"I was walking toward Spitz's parents' place and I saw this crowd collecting near the building and then I saw this body under a white sheet, and it was Spitz. There was blood all over the ground. I was too upset to meet her family, to do anything; I started walking home. I remember: I was on 55th Street between Second and Third I think, we can check that out later, this orange purple sun had just sunk behind a building. I was thinking of Spitz, how soft her lips were, and of robbers. As I stared at this brown building which looked like a building I had just dreamt about, I heard footsteps behind me. For some strange reason I was scared; incipient New York paranoia; I turned my head . . ."

"What else do you remember?"

My head's throbbing. It's going to burst and I'll be a bunch of shattered bones, blood, and skin.

"When you were at the scene of the crime, or at any other time, do you remember telling anyone Spitz had hired you? Do you remember seeing any of Spitz's family, if you could tell, or asking anyone about Spitz's father?"

I don't want to answer this lunatic's questions. I start speaking, "I was probably mugged by a rapist-murderer-fiend. Wait. I was screaming like a loony when I had found out Spitz was the corpse that I'd avenge Spitz and I asked some cop if he knew Spitz's father."

"Did anyone overhear you?" Peter Peter whispers.

"Sure, all of New York, all the murderers and pickpockets. I was screaming my bloody ass off."

"That's it! Now you've definitely got to quit this detective business!"

"Not on your fucking life."

"Don't you see. Someone heard you ask about Spitz's father and was warning you not to get too curious. You might end up being more than beaten up."

"Everyone gets beaten up in New York. I'm a detective and I'm going to stay a detective. I'm not going to quit my first job." I'm getting all fired up, the hell with my sore head. My head hurts worse than ever. "First I have to get in touch with Spitz's family, try to meet them, find out what's going on. I'll say I'm Spitz's friend."

"Promise me you'll be careful."

I reach for the phone. "Hello," I say in my sweet little-girl voice, "could I please speak to Sally?"

A haughty, slightly cracked woman's voice answers. "I'm sorry, you can't. My only daughter's dead."

"What . . . Sally's dead? Why I just saw her three days ago; she said for me to call I . . ."

"Were you a close friend of hers?"

"Yes. My name's Rip-off Red. I'm a detective; I . . ."

"A detective?" I hear a strange note in her voice. Is she scared, or just curious. "That's strange. Listen, I'd like to meet any close friend of my daughter's. I'm rather distraught now as you can imagine. Listen. Two days from now I'm giving my husband a large party. It's his birthday and unfortunately I can't cancel the party at this late date. Perhaps it's better that it goes on." She sighs.

"If you'd like to come, you're more than welcome."

"Thank you very much Mrs. Spitz. At this time I'd consider myself very fortunate to meet Sally's parents."

"You know our address?"

"Yes, thank you very much, and please accept my deepest sympathy for the unfortunate loss you're bearing."

Phew. "O.K. Two days from now, Peter Peter, I've got a date at Spitz's parents' house. Meet the whole crew."

"What will I do?"

"We've got two days. Tonight I'm going to follow the father if and when he leaves on his nightly fling. When I'm at the party, I want you to watch downstairs and follow the father if he goes anywhere. So we'll have two chances to tie this bird's feathers. I don't want these guys to recognize us yet as a team.

"I told the mother I was a detective to test her: whether she cared I was a detective, whether she showed any signs of fear. She seemed nervous as hell." My head's spinning like I'm going crazy. "Do you want to fuck?" I ask Peter Peter.

"You'd better get some sleep."

"Don't you want to fuck . . ." I feel the blackness getting deeper; the knife is shining in the distance.

"Go to sleep, you need to go to sleep."

I'm in London; I'm walking through the center of a wide street. People run past me, screaming. I look back through the wet gray air; in the distance I see a pale white body writhe on the ground. Slowly the thing lifts its head. It stares at me malevolently, and starts wriggling toward me. I stare at its awful head; I can't find its eyes. I have to run but I can't. It opens its huge jaws sharp white teeth a white tongue darts in and out. I start to run through the long street. The snake starts to move forward. I'm safe; it's moving slowly. I run faster, faster, after three streets I look back to see how much distance I've put between me and the snake. The snake is only a block away from me. I run extremely fast; the faster I run, the closer the snake writhes toward me. The worst evil I know. I feel the snake's breath on my neck I'm so close I can see through its jelly head.

I'm in a cream-white bedroom; a house which looks like this:

LEFT	?	bathroom or bedroom		RIGHT
	bed-room	hall	?	
			bed-	
	?		room	
	kit-chen	living room		

Winnie's bedroom is either the bathroom or the bedroom on the right. We're standing in a huge room, high creamy walls. In the middle of the room, to my right, there's a three-person bed. On the opposite wall above me I see a huge mirror. The rug under my feet is cream-colored. Winnie's immensely rich; we pass time by trying on her clothes. I lie in her bed, wonder which of the gorgeous clothes I should wear: a pink fur ostrich gown, a Victorian lace man's suit. I look up at Winnie who's leaning against the dresser by the bed. No, I remember, she doesn't want to sleep with me.

"Do you want to fuck me?" I ask.

She looks down at me, puts her hand on my head.

I'm lying in bed, the bedroom to the right in the same house, my parents' house. My sister's bedroom is the upper half of the kitchen, a real bedroom. My parents ask her if she wants to fuck me or the governess. She becomes Spitz. She wants to sleep in the governess's bedroom, the bedroom on the left. Spitz and my sister are in bed, fucking. I lie alone in bed: a young boy lies in the twin bed next to mine. He becomes a man and sticks a knife in me. Light gathers around my head; the ceiling flashes on and off. He pulls out the knife and starts to lick it.

I have my hand on Peter Peter's cock. I don't want to fuck. Peter Peter's reading a book, *The Complete Stories of Sherlock Holmes;* the corner of the book sticks into my back. He rubs my head and continues reading. I take out a sheet of paper on which I've written down all the past events concerning Spitz; I'm thinking hard; my hand moves in back of me, up and down Peter Peter's cock. The air's turning dark. I bring my hand to my mouth, spit in it so it can move more easily; start rubbing Peter Peter again. Of course I don't notice what I'm doing.

I can't feel the wrinkles in Peter Peter's cock anymore. It's beginning to jut against my ass. I continue to stroke him; now I concentrate on the stroking and forget I'm a detective. At first I move my hand slowly, very steadily; then I increase the speed of the hand's movement; his cock begins to throb. I try to match the rhythm of my hand's movement with the rhythm of the throbbing. Peter Peter's still reading his book.

"Do you want to fuck?"

"I don't want to hurt you."

I take my hand off his cock and grab his hand. I let his middle fingers stroke the delicate opening of my ass. He turns me over on my back; he rolls on me, letting all the covers twist to the right. I'm freezing. I carefully arrange the covers over his back cuddle him with my arms he slips his left hand under my right buttock, and slips his finger into my open wet asshole. A second of pain then throbbing pleasure. His cock jerks at my cunt. I let the pleasure overwhelm me I wait until I can't wait any longer; suddenly I swerve around, stick my belly into the bed, jut my ass against Peter Peter's cock.

"Is this going to hurt you?"

My leg and thigh muscles tense. I close my eyes as if I'm receiving a shot. I can feel nothing. Peter Peter's cock thrusts into my ass. He's too big; I can't possibly keep him in my ass. He's very still; he waits until every one of my muscles relaxes. He begins to move a bit, a half-inch, then an inch, back and forth; I feel pain mingle with pleasure as my thighs and buttocks start moving with him, he moves slightly faster, slightly longer strokes. Each time his cock moves farther inside me, my clit begins to swell. I have a pleasurable sore between my legs, a multisensitive nipple which, the more it's caressed, the more it wants. I turn my head to the side and see Peter Peter's huge blue eyes. He starts to move faster; the bed shakes; the room begins to tremble; he puts his hands on my thighs to keep them still so he can hit me as hard and deep as possible. My clit swells to enormous proportions it's about to burst fires swirl through my whole body. His cock begins to tremble, I get scared I won't come; his cock grows and grows. Now there's no pain, a muscle inside my ass begins to tremble; just as he reaches the height of speed, long stroke; all the walls of flesh inside my ass tremble explode. Jewels.

We fall into an endless sleep.

The clock rings 9:00. An hour to get to the house at 57th Street and First to trace where Spitz's father goes at 10:00. I decide to dress as a top-class whore; no cop will bother me. I put on slight makeup, lilac suede shoes like thirties' sandals which are surprisingly comfortable to walk in, a black wool dress whose back begins at my ass and ends at mid-calf, a black wool scarf wrapped around my neck and falling to my legs, mink around my shoulders. Now I'm ready for the night.

By 10:00 I'm inconspicuously waiting in the doorway of the building next to the 410 building, as if for a cab. The doorman, my friend with the aid of a ten-dollar tip, clues me that Mr. Spitz has just appeared. "There he is, lady. Hope you get him where you want him."

He's a tall man, about 50 years old, bald head, on the heavy side though might have once been an athlete, a largish nose. He picks up a paper and puts it under his arm. I keep about a block away from him; in this ritzy neighborhood, there's hardly anyone on the streets this time of night. The city's beautiful at night: the lights show and hide all of the darkening streets. The cops have disappeared and the anarchists come out. Spitz walks down First Avenue, past drugstores, two dress stores, a bunch of high-class bars. By now we're crossing 55th Street. He stops and looks at his watch; I look around. I slink further into the shadows. Black figures pass by me; in the darkness a car honks and races down the street, a Rolls-Royce or a Bentley. In between avenues there are no streetlights and only one light on each corner of the avenues. I see a man standing by a car, one of his hands stuck between the glass of the window and the top of the car's window. I slink by him, anonymous. A woman in a white hat stops Spitz and briefly talks to him. He nods, continues walking down First Avenue. Does she have any connection to Sally's death? We walk past secondhand bookstores, a candy store. He's walking fast, but not hurrying. A black man in a black night.

10:20. Just as I begin to think there's nothing to this story, Spitz turns into a fancy bar. The Irish Saloon. Now we're between 50th and 51st Street. Diplomats' district. I wait outside the saloon, thinking the old guy's just getting a drink. Five minutes. Ten minutes go by. At 10:35 I walk into the saloon. Beneath dim red lights guys in black overcoats and jackets are sitting on bar stools sharing cigarettes and probably political secrets. A woman with a veil over her face is staring at me. No sign of Spitz. I walk over to the tables; look around; hang around the bathrooms as long as I dare. I walk over to the bartender.

"Seen a guy around here, about 50, bald, dark overcoat, large nose?"

"A few of them. One just got a drink about ten minutes ago, and left somewhere."

I walk slowly out to the dark street. No signs of Spitz's father. A tall woman who looks like Spitz passes me by. As a superdetective I know I'm a failure. It's getting more and more complicated.

5. May 1

Peter Peter and I sleep through all of Tuesday except for the five hours in which we fuck. My bruises disappear.

6. May 2

I become a murderess

In my velvet and sapphire gown, I ring a doorbell in this apartment house. An invisible hand opens the door and I walk in. No one says anything to me; they're all too busy drinking and walking around. I can't see anyone. I start fantasizing that a beautiful man or woman walks up to me, takes my hand, and leads me to a corner by a window where everyone's disappeared. The room's completely black. The stranger looks into my eyes, promises me money, fame, and undying affection; I fall madly in love. My blood rushes into my cunt. Our hands mingle, all the liquids of my body swirl back and forth, I can't see I feel the other body throb we slowly sink into a berserk caress. A hand grabs my hand: "You're Red, aren't you? My name's Loulou."

I look up into the eyes of a tall dark-haired woman. Her eyes are brown, high cheekbones, her mouth is thin and red. She's wearing a black velvet coat over a black turtleneck, and striped red velvet pants, black tights. I don't want to know who she is.

Her grip on my hand tightens; she leads me over to a dark corner, not saying a word, and smiles at me. Our legs brush against each other. As my free hand reaches up to stroke her cheek, her hand lets go of my hand; she puts her hands around the lower half of my face, lifts my face up to hers and stares at me. I'm not able to look back at her. Her right leg works between my legs. My mouth starts to tremble, she bends down to me and with one hand on the back of my neck to steady my head, places her mouth against mine. I feel two thin pressures of flesh, then a tongue, like a thin living needle trying to burn out my tongue. She raises her head, stares at me, and walks away.

A thin man, tall, with a large nose, is standing next to me. It's Spitz's father. "You must be Miss Red." He takes a trembling hand and offers it to me. "Sally told me before she died that you were good friends." He starts sniffling. "Now that she's gone, all I can do is talk to her friends. You have to tell me everything you two did together." He starts to tremble, and his voice goes up three octaves. "My wife should have canceled this party; she does too much for me. I work so hard, I never have time to rest, and now some, some thug murders my daughter, my only child. It's the duty of the police to kill every dope-fiend they see. It's a crime for innocent hard-working citizens to be continuously in fear of these thugs. It's a goddamn crime I tell you." He slaps the table. "I have to be careful of my heart, my doctor won't allow me to be scared; I have to be sure I'm not chilled. I'm not allowed to exercise, or to eat any harsh food like pork or lamb. I could die very easily."

I wonder how he could have gotten away from me, my superb tail job.

"Sally was such a dear child; she was always so loving and gentle to her father. She never tried to assert herself or to go directly against my wishes. She was always smiling and had lots of friends. But, of course, you know that." Spit starts drooling out of his mouth. "She wasn't interested in getting married or becoming a secretary, but I'm sure she would have changed in time when she began to realize the harsher realities of life. I always gave her the best schooling and doctors I could afford. She had everything a little girl could want."

I have to get away. He couldn't possibly be a villain, only a dupe. His eyes begin to glitter.

"Of course, you have to meet my wife and Julie, our dear friend. You'll want to meet all the family. I'll look for my dear wife and tell her you're here."

I fall into a drunken sleep.

I'm standing alone in the corner of a room full of murderers. The murderers slowly pale into a thin blue light which swirls up my cunt. My hand falls against my cunt.

Peter Peter takes the clock and disappears. I can feel my hand pressing below the bone at the top of my cunt. I want to move my hand lower but don't want these people to see me. There are no people in the room. A tall man walks toward me; his face is thin and his nose is large. As he walks toward me, he becomes larger and larger until he's over six feet tall. I think that he's Sherlock Holmes. By now, my hand is between my legs: fingers press the black velvet into my cunt, slowly and rhythmically. The man and I are standing, a foot apart, in the middle of the room. The man reaches into the pocket of his cape, takes out a velvet Moroccan case, a book of matches, a small jar containing white liquid, and a spoon. He pours some of the liquid into the spoon, holds a match under the spoon until the liquid in the spoon begins to bubble. He blows out the match. He opens the velvet case, takes out a hypodermic syringe, then a clean needle, fits the needle in the syringe; he draws the liquid into the syringe. I breathe harder. He rolls up his shirt sleeve, extends a white arm. Tiny puncture marks cover his wrist and arm. He takes a long time finding a new space; finds one, sticks the needle into his arm, presses on the plunger. Blood spurts into the syringe. I watch him carefully. The more stationary and lifeless he becomes, the more rapidly my fingers move. It's as if I'm watching a snake.

He looks at me and holds the needle up toward my face. This is the most famous detective, and I have to fuck him. I walk toward the needle: when I'm almost touching his arm, Sherlock grabs my arm and swirls me around. His arm extends out straight;

his finger points at some person. I think it's a man. The person quickly sneaks behind a piece of furniture. I can tell I'm drunk. My fingers are making my clit into a piece of white burning coal and yet I'm unable to come. The needle hangs in the air; its tip begins to waver and to turn around as if it's seeking someone. It stops and points to a figure, again I think, the figure of a man: this time a shorter person. I'm hopelessly drunk, or else a clairvoyant. Ha. I want some guy to come to me: to put one arm around my waist, one arm around my shoulders, to draw me to him and hold me until my breath disappears. I want him to put his lips on my lips simultaneously his hand over my cunt so that he convinces me to fuck him. Slowly his hands pull up my long velvet skirt, and his fingernails scratch my legs. I thrust my thighs against his cock I feel his cock harden, begin to move into me. His fingers enter my cunt I know I've found Prince Charming flames burst from the upper arcs of my legs. My gums and nipples and cunt grow wet and tender. I want him to take his hands, to thrust them hard under my thighs, to raise my thighs up to his wet mouth, to ease my ache with his tongue and teeth and lips all trembling shaking furiously. He'll have to bring me fame and fortune. He places his hands under my thighs. I let my weight fall on my calves and feet; I squeeze my knees around his thick open mouth. I lift up my thighs; he lowers his mouth, suddenly sticks his tongue into my open ass. His tongue feels strange; as he moves his tongue slowly from my ass down to my clit, the lines of nerves from my ass to my clit to my spine start to tingle, vibrate harder and harder as he gently moves my hair away, touches his tongue against my million-times aching clit. Just enough to tease my clit; to keep my nerves aching. He presses his teeth against my clit, begins to suck, harder and harder; my clit swells without helping me come. I thrash around; I get angry; I'm never going to ease my burning and lust; I dig my fingers and fingernails into his head: scratch; he bites and nibbles me harder. I can't stand this. I lift my thighs higher I twist like a shot animal. His long tongue touches my clit stops touches my clit stops darts over the clit now harder now harder I start screaming madly I clench my hands into his head he presses his tongue deep into my cunt swollen leaps at my clit hits it. As I come, moving my fingers, drunk as any rich biddy, I remember how sweet I felt pressing my mouth against Spitz's cunt wet in the godforsaken airplane bathroom.

I'm standing alone in this semidark living room. I'd better get a drink. I stumble to the bar, grab some booze, and look around. No one seems to have noticed my little sexual adventures. Bodies lay strewn over the floor; a few stout hearts bumble around with their drinks. For all I know, I could be dreaming.

A thin dark man in green corduroy pants walks up to me and slaps me on the back. At least here's someone who treats me with respect. "Hello, Red, you don't mind if I call you Red; I'm Julie."

Is he another suspect, or someone I have to avoid? I take a chance and smile. Anyway, I like the guy.

"I'm Julie: I'm very charming and very good in bed."

I bow delightedly.

"It's only an invitation, I don't know if you're terribly interested in men. O," he turns around and leads another person up to me, "let me introduce Sally's mother to you. She's also my lover. Or mistress, if that's what you call it."

I look up at a tall woman who has dark hair. For the first time tonight, I'm surprised: "Your name is Loulou."

She smiles at me, and puts her arm around my waist. Julie also smiles and wiggles away.

"We must have a lot we have to discuss." She takes my hand and leads me up the white staircase to the hidden rooms. I'm under a hypnotic spell. We walk arm-in-arm into a pale-gray, almost silver room. Blue and gold draperies hang over the ceiling and walls; pearl carvings fall down from the ceilings and cover inlaid shelves. I feel as if I'm in the middle of a cavern. She holds up two glasses, each filled with a violet liquid, and hands one of them to me. Am I being poisoned? I sip down the liquid, and look at her. She lies on a huge bed, the upper half of her body leans against three pale giant pillows. We stare at each other. I throw off my shoes; then lift up my velvet dress from the floor, twist it in my hands over my head. I hold my hands under my breasts, lifting up my breasts, and arching my back away from her. Would she have murdered her only child? She draws me onto the bed. She takes my face in her hands, as she did the first time, and presses my head to her breast. She wraps her arms around my back and head, throws a leg over my thighs; I catch her soft nipple in my mouth. For hours I suck free of constraint, free of any fear. I close my hands around her thin back; I ride up her body until my cunt mashes against her cunt I lash at her face with my tongue my long fingernails carve red streaks into her skin. Her eyes open wider, she loves me, I jut my knee against her cunt I move my knee thrust my hand into her cunt take it out thrust again I can feel her begin to feel to worship me I thrust at her with my whole body. I place my thumb on her clit, two fingers in her uterus, the other hand teases the thin nerves of her ass; we're mirrors in this silver cavern: each of our orgasms is double I put my leg over my thumb with my whole body I begin to ride into her her breaths become rasps her fingernails dig into my spine her clit wriggles under my fingers I throw myself at her I command her to obey this rapid rhythm I command her to scream to sink down into ecstasy I tell her I'll do anything I have to have her orgasm beneath my fingers liquid comes out of her cunt her breathing becomes electric; as I begin to pulse desire, her whole body tenses relaxes tenses tenses, and shudders. My hand gently rubs her clit until she lies still.

We lie together; we look into each other's face. I feel my body is almost rigid, the muscles around my cunt are strained and tense. She holds me, kisses my damp forehead; she gets up from the huge bed to fuck me. I lie on my back watching the ceiling, the shadows of our arms pass across it the arms of maniacs: I'm waiting for her. I look up at her face, at her huge eyes which mirror me I want her to possess me, to enrage me my muscles are quivering; I look up at her face I touch her falling breasts and nipples with my right hand I touch her low white belly the white skin beneath her breasts which now shows I cry to her, and moan. She takes out from under the bed a huge instrument, straps black leather bands around her waist, she fills herself and fondles her new cunt I look up at her she checks her temperature, slowly, come down over me. As I feel her enter me, I feel her fucking me a double female, and open my legs wider I expand to enormous proportions: I can't find her I have to find her I spread my legs wider and wider as my whole body is opening I find her cock I come a few times I yell and kiss her thin ears and the skin of her face. She unstraps her cock and we fall into a light sleep. I'm some fine detective.

The murder suspect opens her eyes. "Go away now, and return the night after tomorrow. I want to be alone with Julie tonight. In two days, if you want, you can see both Julie and me."

"Can I bring a friend?"

She doesn't answer. I'm still drunk; I want to go to sleep. I can't figure this dame out. And she's much too dangerous for me to fool with, not that I'm going to stop. I wonder if she killed her daughter and if so, why. Is she trying to get hold of the family money? I didn't get to see much of the party with all the sex stuff.

"Where does your husband go at 10:00 every night; who does he make those mysterious checks out to?"

"How should I know? That's what I want you to find out." That's reasonable.

"Should I find out who killed your daughter?"

We smile at each other. She pulls me to her and kisses me, with her thick wet lips inside me, and her tongue. If she's trying to make me unsuspect her, she's succeeding.

Loulou, Julie, and the vegetable father. I wonder who else I have to meet.

Whoever else you want to fuck.

I slip my velvet and sapphire gown over my head and step out into the night.

Part Two

7.

Henriette Cailloux
1878–1943 brown hair brown eyes France.
shoots and kills a newspaperman who's threatening her husband's
    political position
is acquitted
Lizzie Borden
1892. Massachusetts. burglaries
butchers with hatchet her mother and father they don't give her
    enough money
dies home 35 years after murders
Jane Cannon Cox
1876. the rich and the near-rich. England.
poisons her friend's and mistress's husband he's planning to kick
    her out
sneaks away to Jamaica
Florence Chandler Maybrick
1871. Liverpool.
possibly poisons (arsenic) her husband who regularly takes drugs
    mainly to get away from him
15 years in prison
Lydia Danbury Sherman
1846. New York. mercy killing.
poisons (arsenic) her husband he's been dropped from the police
    force is miserable.

2 years after husband dies poisons her son and younger daughter. they have no father.

poisons oldest daughter when daughter has typhoid. poisons other two children. kills next two husbands and some of their children one for money.

kills child to hurt husband.

imprisoned for life.

Madeleine Hamilton Smith

1855. Scotland.

poisons (arsenic) an old lover who's trying to prevent her marrying another man. she has money.

dies when 92.

Maria Marten.

1826. Polsted.

She and lover William Corder kill illegitimate child. William Corder kills her she wants to marry him blackmail.

Adelaide Blanche de la Tremouille.

1875. England.

poisons (chloroform) her husband. ménage à trois he wants to fuck her first time ever 11 years marriage

dies in an operation

Laura Lane Fair.

1837. America. Nevada during the gold rush.

kills a Yankee who raises a Union flag over her hotel.

Crittenden gets her acquitted.

shoots to kill Crittenden who's giving her shit promising to marry her while already married 7 years

82 years old dies starving girl of the golden West.

Mary Ann Cotton

1872. Durham.

poisons 3 husbands, 18 children, her mother, a husband's sister, a lodger

hangs.

Charlotte Wood alias Henrietta Robinson
1853. New York.
poisons a low-class family revenge herself against her rich parents
    everyone denies her
imprisoned in Sing Sing for life.

On the 18th of August I become a murderer. I've taken too much shit in this empire city: Spitz's death three knifings in my side; I decide to revenge myself! Protect myself! I'll get Spitz's murderer, whoever's rooking Spitz's father, the strange way. I become completely elegant.

You see,

I have a dream. A world of delight birds sing to a real sun in a real city no one leaves out anybody. Everyone does what he she wants. A materialist revolution is happening: whatever you have you get more. Everyone is a Rockefeller only everyone is a real person everyone steals jewels gold bars opens banks heists trains hauls narcotics masturbates. There are no more moralists.

This is the diary of Rip-off Red's childhood, of how she becomes a murderer, a sneak, a thief. You have to understand her humble beginnings, how she rose from the gutter; how at first people disown her, deny her; how as she grows stronger and wilier they begin to accept her, finally love her and her strange actions. As she grows older, her actions become stranger and stranger; by the time she meets Sally Spitz, she's a total genius.

Listen, find out why she avenges Sally's murder, why she clears up the mystery of Sally's father, though she won't do this until the end, why she becomes the world's foremost and fiercest murderess. Why I become, shitheads, the greatest murderess (and detective) in the world:

8.

Ages 1 through 10

I'm born with a diamond in my navel which old women say means good luck. Good luck or not, when I'm only a week old, my mother cuts out the diamond and sells it for a few hundred less than she hoped. That's the first money my parents steal from me.

My father's name is Oiving and my mother's, Clear. She always wanted to stop being Jewish. When my mother's father sold the monopoly he had established during World War II, getting control of the black market sugar, selling it to Jews at exorbitant rates, my parents of course were Jewish but they were doing their best to buy their way into Gentile society (while they still had the money to hope) in 1951, he cleared a million; half of the million goes to his wife, my mother's mother; half of it is split between my mother, my sister, and me. My mother gives her share of the loot back to mama so mama will keep supporting her. And she does. They're a cute couple. Grandpa, the brains of the family, dies in 1953. My sister's and my money's held in trust by some ghost.

My mother and adopted father gradually use up my and my sister's money trying to get to know Rockefeller and Ford. Not having any taste, courage, or enough evil in them, they don't succeed. They also lose most of their money, and move from ritzy Prospect Park section in Brooklyn and a Rolls-Royce to a middle-class dump in Queens. My adopted father's in the ladies' gloves business; I'm 7 years old.

During the era of their affluence and wealth, I remember mainly my grandmother, the queen dyke of the family. She has an apartment in an old hotel in New York, around the corner from the Museum of Modern Art. Three rooms: one of the rooms, her workroom where she writes dirty poems, is gray and black. Gray walls, black bookcases, desk, table, red pillows, very suave. Huge pearls inside jars filled with transparent poisonous liquids. Tiny Chinese and Japanese dolls with intricately embroidered layers of orange and gold silk over their black-and-white bodies. Books with strange pictures and red velvet covers which teach me most of what I know at this early age.

The ceiling, floor, and walls of the winding hall are tiny mirrors placed against each other. I dance through this hall, twist my body into impossible positions, and become a hundred kinds of criminals. The hall leads to the living room, the main room, where everything's yellow: a huge yellow couch with cushions three feet thick; I throw myself onto the couch, past two tiny footstools, I sink into the soft cloth down below the wood edge of the frame. Over the couch there's a large picture of an African woman. I remember staring at her large round breasts which hung low, as mine now are, and the green cloth around her thighs. On a table carved out of two kinds of glittering wood's a silver teapot and burner. Tiny flowers and cupids carve into the silver. A wood desk hides the southwest wall of the room; it has tiny compartments into which ivory women figures and notebooks with strange inkblots are jammed.

The bedroom's the most fantastic of the rooms. I used to sit or hide for hours on a thick blue satin chaise longue; I cover my body, no matter what the temperature of the room, with a huge blue satin quilt. Or I run behind the white silk curtains; I peer into the closet as big as a room; I go into the second bathroom to stare at the rows of yellow and brown perfumes. A triple-person bed takes up most of the space of the bedroom; over the bed, a huge pearl fan. Pictures containing different layers of carved ivory depicting justice lie on top of curling white wood cabinets. Actually the room was hideous.

Before I had to exile myself from New York from this disgusting crap, this room is what I remember. Otherwise the only decent part of my childhood was my dreams. My grandmother suited this room and my dreams. She imitated senility when it pleased her so she could do exactly what she wanted. My sister and I used to follow her into the neighboring stationery store. She'd order the owner of the store to bring her Scotch tape, order my sister to take the Scotch tape, walk out of the store. We were always sure to keep some of our allowance for emergencies, whatever part of the allowance our mother hadn't stolen.

She'd steal sugar from restaurants, blankets and toilet paper from the hotel in which she lived. She had been born into a poor family and in this land of opportunities married rich. She never forgot it. She kept trying to palm a black seal coat off on me until I lost my so-called virginity and was too old for it. My mother was jealous.

My mother used to dress me up like a 1930s Shirley Temple; even then I had the sense to be suitably embarrassed. She'd curl my hair into repulsive cutie-pie peaks, blot red lipstick on me, paste pink organdy, the newest thing my dears, on my anemic thighs and invisible cunt. She'd drag me out of hiding from the bathroom. And darling white gloves from my father's factory to protect my sweet lady's hands. Finally, on my eighth birthday, she sticks me into a girdle with pink flowers sewn on it and taxis me to The Hotel Grift for a birthday party. The whole family walks together step by step into the downstairs dining room; my grandmother lifts up my pink dress to show the headwaiter my new girdle. New York lechers. I hate this part of my life.

Enough of the childhood business. So this wonderful grandmother and her daughter steal all my money, steal all my sister's,

Sweetie-pie's, money, spend all the money on the Gentiles, and we end up on Dirt Row in Queens.

When I'm six years old, actually, we move from Brooklyn ritz to New York nouveau-Jew-ritz: Park Avenue and 72nd Street. They send me for two years to this up-and-coming or just coming ladies' school: the Ox School, just down the street from where we live, across the street from the Rockefeller mansion. The teachers in the school do their best to program me to be a good little lady; I couldn't care less. By this time, I've got a gang. When I'm six I'm being a nuisance because I read too much, so my mother tells me to play downstairs. Trembling, frightened I'll have to talk to anyone my own age outside of school, I go downstairs, meet Mag and Phyllis, two charming brats my own age. We play handball, establish a gang in which a kid can enter only by completely stripping in front of us on a rainy day in Central Park, steal sex magazines. For bigger kicks, we stop distinguished old gentlemen on the street and ask them to tell us what a "penis" is. They usually do. Kids get bored as easily as adults. This is the old days of New York when a child could walk safely down a New York street, a New York street in the rich ghettoes, and wouldn't get busted or raped. Rich people still took taxis. I still wasn't sure of my sex.

So the family goes broke, or whatever the rich call "broke" which isn't by my rip-off standards today *Broke,* and when I'm 8½ years old, we move to Queens. etc. etc. Narratives you know are purely for shit. Here's the information go fuck yourself. I enter some miserable P.S. 69 School, meet males my own age; most important, I get my own real New York gang, The Banana Followers, and finally, I come. *This is the beginning:*

Meanwhile, I still don't know how I've been rooked out of my money. I'm an innocent dope. I think my parents are wonderful even if my adopted father doesn't notice me because he's too stupid and my mother's always talking on the telephone and stealing my money. I don't even know yet that money exists. Except when my mother tells my adopted father she's supporting us and him and he's not able to do anything. But he picks up her slippers well. My sister and I know how to hide.

I meet Harvey the Bagel and Weirdo the Rat. I'm Tough Turk. We three form the nucleus of The Banana Followers: our territory ranges from Kissena Boulevard to Jackson Avenue. Anyone who dares enter our territory has to show a special pass which contains a streak of our blood. Our main enemy is The Tomatoes, a gang of chain boys. I learn to use the switchblade, the top of the garbage can, and karate, to run from all cops, and in cases of dire need, to cry. I don't give a shit about school. Harvey and Weirdo become my closest friends; they even send me a bottle of piss on my wedding day. By now, they're sitting in jail, trying to plan the Great Train Bombing of 1974. When we're not fighting, we get stoned. On January 5, 1958 The Banana Followers and The Tomatoes have their major fight. Louie the Lip had been pestering us for a few days; he was hankering after our stored-up Thunderbird. He was a mean son-of-a-bitch; he even wore his mother's apron to show he could take anything. I was playing pool, trying for the first time in my life to earn some honest money. I see Louie coming around the corner.

"Harvey, Weirdo," I say, "here's a guy who doesn't have a pass."

Three filthy heads swing around simultaneously. I pick up my money, walk out the door. I know my boys are behind me.

"Can I help you Louie?"

He doesn't answer me, walks ahead, looks around, turns back, leaves the street. We go back to playing pool.

We play for an hour; talk about various gang matters. Another dame wants to enter the gang: Margie Mintz. That's O.K. with me as long as she changes her name.

"Look around," says Weirdo, "not too fast." I slowly turn my head, see Louie's prominent lurch.

"What that fatherfuck want now?"

"I think he's asking us to help him."

We rise up, pocket our weapons; leave the pool hall. The sky's yellow. We walk slowly toward Louie.

"You need help again, Lip."

The Lip again ignores us, walks past Weirdo, past me, past Harvey. Maybe he's strung out. Just as he walks past Harvey again, Harvey shoots out a leg. Trip. Lip gets up, whistles, from around the corner come thousands of filthy disgusting chain boys. The Tomatoes. I grab a steel can top as a shield, duck from two knives; I see Harvey and Wierdo have done the same. One Tomato rushes me; I knee him BOOM I clobber a second as he goes to knife me. Out of the corner of my eye I see Harvey's gotten three down, on his fourth. Can't let my attention wander; I throw one creep over my back. Even if we're the better fighters, there's too many of them.

"Hey Weirdo they're too many. We'll have to use Plan Number 1."

Weirdo and I rush back out of the crowd to an improvised platform made of wooden crates. Harvey can take care of himself. We throw off our clothes; we don't have much time and we've never done this before; Weirdo's about two inches taller than me. He places his hands on my shoulders, gives me the signal that everything's O.K. I lie ass down on the wooden crates; I'm too excited to feel the splinters entering my soft child's skin. Suddenly I feel two warm objects touch my lips, my whole body starts to shake from the intensity of the touch. As Weirdo's tongue enters my mouth, the bars of my stomach open, disappear; I feel like water an explosion happens his mouth lifts up his lips crawl to the left side of my mouth, across my cheek to my ear. His teeth start to nibble at my left earlobe he does something now I think that he had started to breathe in my ear warm shivers go up down my spine a hand's under my skin shaking me I kiss his cheek his eye his eyelash I've got no more sight I can feel his body begin to tremble I only remember sensation a wet thing in my ear an explosion in my abdomen start I again I relax enough to become aware of Weirdo's body his hand reaches down to my skinny hand takes hold of it places it on a hard cylindrical limb or something between our stomachs. I feel strange nauseous touching this thing I don't exactly understand what's happening but I think we might be fucking which I'm not supposed to do I do everything I'm not supposed to do. I tighten my hand around his thing, I can hear his breathing grow harsher harsher the thing in my hand moves grows ooch I don't feel disgusted suddenly the inside of my belly begins to tingle grows very sensitive below I want to feel pressure I raise up my thighs so his hard thing will press me right I raise up higher higher he breathes like a crazy bum I take a hand jam three of his fingers into where I piss explosions burst out all over my thighs throughout my stomach WOW he shakes the thing against my stomach quivers, leaves a thick white foam on my white skin.

I wonder if we just fucked. Weirdo and I raise our heads. Everyone's disappeared. The Tomatoes are gone; we've foiled them. Ha. Ha. Ha. Five bodies lie strewn on the ground. We hear a strange noise, look around. Harvey the Bagel's to our right, a broomstick in his hand, leaping up and down, screeching.

"We beat 'em, we beat 'em. The plan worked."

"O.K. boys," I stand up, rub the white foam into my stomach, and start putting my clothes on. Weirdo grins madly, and does the same. "Let's go steal some Thunderbird."

9.

Age 11

I'm lying in bed in a dark green room a slim bed next to the wall. I stick my second finger into my nose, feel around for the little bumps of yellow; each time I find a bump, or better, a wet glop, I rub it from my finger onto my lip until the dry specks roll off my lips. I move my hand to my breasts, hardly breasts, but two areas of softness separated by a wide bone. I wonder when I'll be old enough to get rid of my parents. My hand slowly strokes the soft curve of my belly one finger dives into my tiny navel that tickles I continue to rub my belly the inner sides of my legs soft as my belly. I bring my hand up to my wet lips coat my third finger with the wetness bring finger to my mouth. Mmm tastes like chocolate cookies, the Nabisco white-filled ones. I don't like cookies. I start to dream I'm Rip-off Red: I'm in a car, a black coach the coach is moving up a hill. On the hill wood wagon wheel tiny wood houses built into the hillside with slanting roofs, a few old-fashioned hotels. Sherlock Holmes sits in the coach, opposite to me, smoking a pipe. I have to find out for him who set fire to the school gym. We go past the main hotel of the mystery which is burning. Red flames. The family want me to find the murderer. Into a dark German forest black trees against black sky; evil children play in this forest, murderer children, terrorist children.

My mother enters the green room. "Is anything bothering you darling?"

"Mommy. Saturday night, I kissed a boy. Was that evil of me?"

She floats over to my bed, sits down next to me.

"Of course not, darling. Don't worry about things like that. It's natural; everyone does them. Always tell me what you're doing."

"I felt so strange," I love to lie to her; I lie all the time; "like I was exploding."

She laughs, and bends down over me. I can see her black hair flashing green eyes. "Tell me, do you do anything else?"

"O no mommy. I don't know what you're talking about." Pause. "Mommy, did you ever kiss men; take their clothes off?"

"I wouldn't do that to my little girl." For the second time her lips brush against my forehead, then my lips. I want her to lay her head against my head, to cover my tense body with her long elegant grown-up body. To make me feel as good as I make myself feel good with my finger, only better, much much better. Then she has to slowly draw down the covers from between our bodies; she has to like a probe draw her tongue between my fur eyebrows around my nose to my full damp lips; with her tongue, lick the insides of my lips, my tender gums between my tongue and my inner cheeks; then like a poison dart, shoot her tongue into my mouth, as far as it goes, the inside of my throat, the melting beginnings of my lungs until my breathing stops.

She lays her head against my head black against brown green eyes against brown eyes I'm being wrapped in a blanket of white velvet skin. Huge animals, black oxen, by black leather straps tied around my thighs, chest, and arms drag me around in thick brown mud puddles; black horses whose manes are endless gallop through the black of the soul. Her tongue touches the root of each curling hair; it cuts through the hairs, finds nothing, suddenly pushes down across my forehead to under my eyes, the heavy shadows, the deep curves of the skin around the cheekbones. She licks each bone, each piece of skin; my face transforms into fire, an animal being taken care of by its mother animal, fed by its mother animal, separated from fear.

"Are you O.K. darling?"

I draw her body closer to me; I put my arms around her back, run my fingers up and down her back; I fell her spine rise above the white silk on her skin. I don't want her to take off her clothes. I follow her: I put my tongue against her two quivering nostrils, then at the top of her lips between the drawn double peaks, I learn every inch of her mouth's warm insides, the damp softness of the sides, the strange roughness of her tongue. Electric bolts blast through my body. I swirl my tongue around the sharp edge of her ear, inside one coil to another coil, a maze in which I lose myself; sharp teeth nibble at the muscles swirling from my shoulder to my neck. What's happening? My body shudders; I follow her: bare my teeth into her tensed shoulder, nibble at the sinew, the tough brown skin; I lick up the salt. She turns, two strange green eyes look at me; a heavy naked body bears down on mine, pressure at the triangle of bones that bear up between our legs, my stomach grows, every inch of skin inside grows unbearably sensitive.

She's putting her two endless arms around me, holding me, I'm the most precious being in the world, I'm the most tender and beautiful; I grasp my wrists with my hands around her back to give myself up to her, so she understands. She places her right hand on my left breast, moves the edge of her hand back and forth so that all my feeling flows into the tip of the flat breast; I arch upwards, I arch into her hand. The palm of her hand presses down touches the sleeping nipple; I've never felt anything like this: the nipple bursts out, aches to be touched, not to be touched. She takes my nipples in her thumbs and second fingers, roll them, lightly brushes them I want to put my hands around her short hair, I want to draw her face slowly slowly toward one of my breasts, to feel her mouth almost touch, touch, wet lips then tongue one of the soft nipples the flat breast, feel the complete weight of her head lying on my chest, my hands in the welter of her hair, rubbing, rubbing, rubbing.

She slowly lowers her head to my chest, toward my breast, her red lips barely touch the reaching nipple brush once! Brush twice! She takes my head in her hands, hands flat over my ears, her eyes open again into mine.

"My child."

She pulls me down; down until my mouth is over her breast, my lips are closing on a hard pointed piece of skin; my tiny tongue licks back forth, not too hard, each lick causes tiny feathers to brush the desire rising in our legs: brush, brush; the muscles in my cheeks and mouth tense, relax in the back of my mouth there's a tiny pipe which sucks in my tongue, the hard skin my tongue's touching. My tongue disappears I'm sucking without breathing; all that matters is the sucking. Two hands at the back of my head, the tips of fingers draw my head closer, into, in the breast; my nose nuzzles against the soft skin. I'm beginning to disintegrate, I awaken my tongue, brush it again against the hardening nipples, I rise up I awake. My two hands travel up down the sides of the body waist in thighs out legs slow very slow I pull myself down against and under, the softness.

Two hands reach under my shoulders, push me up again so my head's on the pillow; they flutter over me, touch me on my shoulders, my underarms, at the side of my calves, between my belly and cunt, below my ribs. My mother murmurs. I don't understand her.

"How am I going to do this? Is she old enough?" She suddenly dives under the covers into the boiling blackness; two hands part my legs; a wet animal scrapes the tender mouth between my legs.

"That hurts." A warm hand presses down on my belly, molds the sensitive desire in my belly; I awaken more; as the desire like a window, a breeze, opens, tiny fingers press and rub the cleavage that separates my belly and the tops of my thighs. The fingers crawl down softly around the triangle that ends my body, a few sea-hairs press lightly again press lightly something between in and outside me, at that edge of my tender opening, begins to throb the hands move down pull at the red lips, caress the muscle below the ass, the delicate skin around the asshole, grow around twice three times my whole lower body is dying to be touched as it was first touched. Again the wet animal, the tongue enters my hair and cunt something hard goes up me; the hurt changes to desire to ease increase the desire does that feel good does that feel good does that feel good I feel only a tiny knob at the beginning of my cunt throbbing I try to imagine my mother she sits in a chair with a glass of champagne in her left hand her lips are dark she's laughing pretending she's a child she's telling me how as a kid she used to sneak down the fire escape from Uncle Ally and Aunt Belladonna to run away with some Gentile boy or her best friend and lover Tough Tits Terri the throbbing disappears returns disappears grows stronger faster I feel rough hair between my fingers I press harder the throbbing spreads . . . at the edge of the descent, no, just at the edge; the throbbing grows even stronger almost out of control I'm at a plateau I have to think about something a light explosions shocks me passes over me the knob begins to burst into flames become the fire under an eighteenth-century witch I'm in the flames I'm descending the explosions increase down to the edge one explosion bursts in my legs simultaneously at the base of my spine voom a high huge burning throb hits the center of my clit my whole shudders I yank my mother's head away from my lips.

She takes my head, pushes me down below her lets my head float below her breast, my mouth clasps her nipple, before I have time to recover. I'm floating below an endless green ocean I become nothing I become whatever happens to pass through me. Up down up down white mountains white rivers white fields white narcotics she lays above me she moves slowly into me she moves slowly into me her hands work rapidly maniacally I can feel them below me I can barely feel her body above me, thrashing I can hardly hear her hoarse sighs her whispers I want her to enter me and come in me. I love my mother. Suddenly her body stiffens her hands stop moving silence she will-lessly trembles falls still. I raise my head kiss the tears on her cheeks and mouth. She puts her arms around me I around her; we separate our bodies and she leaves.

White clouds above me; white clouds float through my bones.

10.

Evidence:

Age 8

My mother tells me why I was born: she had a pain in her stomach, it was during the war, she went to some quack doctor (she had just married this guy because the war was happening and she loved his parents); the doctor said she should get pregnant to cure the pain. Since she's married, she gets pregnant, but the pain stays. She won't get an abortion because she's too scared. She runs to the toilet: she thinks she has to shit: I come out. The next day, she has appendicitis.

My mother puts on black fur-lined boots with two-inch pointed heels over her tan stockings, an orange-brown tight sweater over a white bra, she has large soft full breasts, a straight orange-brown skirt with brown and blue triangles above her crotch. Bright red lipstick and pink powder. Over this, her black seal coat. She looks young and pretty. We go out of the apartment together, down to the street where it's snowing, three blocks away to my favorite park. Pure white's covered over the lower level: the basketball court, skating rink, and adult swings, completely; the upper level where seesaws jungle gyms sandboxes used to be, looks like a magic woods. My mother and I play together: she tells me she's my sister. We go to a drugstore to drink ice-cream sodas; a man at the counter asks her if we're sisters.

My mother tells me my "father" isn't my real father: my real father left her when she was three months pregnant; he wanted nothing to do with either of us, ever. This husband has adopted me. That's all she tells me. I feel happy I have none of this father's blood in me.

Age 10

My mother tells me carrot juice is going to come out of me where I piss sometime soon and I shouldn't get worried. All young girls, eventually, once a month, watch carrot juice flow out of their piss-holes. I wonder if I can drink it, and if my mother's lying some more.

Age 11

I see my mother constantly naked: large heavy breasts, violet large nipples whose points are small, large ass and thighs the skin thick and wrinkly, the waist of a boy, extremely short dark dark brown hair, green eyes which can strangely change color, a petulant mouth. She walks back and forth past me to the bathroom.

My mother tells me she hates my real childhood name, only gave me that name because she didn't think at the time it was legal right to give me my nickname. Her husband's sister who is crazy and whom she hates has my real name. She always calls me by my childhood nickname as does everyone I know: institutions at this time call me by my real childhood name.

My mother and my sister lie together on my mother's bed watching TV I sit on the floor in front of my mother's bed. I love the floor. Later I learn to love walls. My father sits on his bed. My mother tells my sister that my father drinks three drinks when he comes home from work, is an alcoholic, falls asleep at 7:30 at night, and never does anything. She tells my sister to laugh at him: my sister laughs at him and tells him he's dull and stupid. He tells me he doesn't know who Dostoyevsky is. My mother tells me she hates his mother because his mother treated her badly when he and my mother first married; my sister and I also have to hate her. My sister laughs. I feel bored.

My mother tells me to wrap my used Kotexes in newspaper. I see dog's turds. Pepper (the dog) takes out a newspaper bundle from the garbage can, chews it up, drags it around the house. My mother sees it: tells me I'm dirty and evil I'm selfish and don't do anything for anyone but myself. She's right.

My mother tells me she loves me and tries to kiss me. I don't tell her I love her. She never does anything for me, and when I want to talk to her, she's always talking to her friends on the telephone. I tell her obviously she doesn't want to talk to me and she tells me I'm a liar. She turns to my sister: asks my sister to play cards with her and fetch her glasses of water, makes my sister her beloved, close friend, and servant.

I dream that my mother's happy again because she has a lover: a tall thin distinguished man who is rough with her which is what she wants. She fucks him and fucks him all the time when my father's gone and when she can sneak out of the house. She now looks beautiful, and she leaves me alone: stops making me do the social things she wants me to do, stops putting me down for my shyness and the ways I act, stops making my life miserable. I see her lying in the tall man's arms, his dark skin next to her paler skin, his mouth moving an inch from hers.

Age 13

I fuck and find out my mother's been lying. I know my mother lies about everything. We outwardly hate each other.

Age 15

My mother tells me to come into her bathroom: she has to talk to me. "How far have you gone with boys? You can't let them touch you there, uh, you know, because then other things will happen, you're disgusting . . ." I interrupt her and say there's no need for her to tell me all this. We don't discuss sex ever again.

One winter afternoon I manage to get out of the house; I take the subway to 9th Street and Third Avenue to see my lover P. We spend the afternoon fucking. When I get home around 6:00 P.M. my mother asks me where I've been. "Just walking around." "Why weren't you at the rehearsal for The Jewish Guild for the Blind dance?" "I'm sorry; I forgot." She starts slapping my face as hard as she can. "WHORE. WHORE."

Age 16
My mother tells me while my father and sister are listening that my father's cock is too wide and short for her and that he doesn't fuck her enough. I show I understand what she means.

Age 17
My father tries to rape me: he thinks that I've been fucking and he starts to cry, puts his arms around me, kisses me, generally glops. I phone my mother who's in their country house, tell her to calm down her husband or I'll never see either of them again. I refuse to kiss him.

The last time I'm home, my mother's giving me trouble: I'm selfish I'm insane I have to see a psychiatrist. I should be dead. I tell her to stop bugging me, I've been having a hard time: I show her my wrists which I've cut up rather badly with razors, trying to punish myself. She tells me not to talk about nasty things at the dinner table.

My mother and I look almost exactly alike; we have many of the same characteristics.

Everything is incredibly beautiful:

I dream that I'm looking out of a window I see a group of

boys playing with each other and laughing. A young boy in a black uniform leaps into the middle of the crowd. I'm not a boy. A servant tells me the boy's planning to bomb the city. Peacocks walk past the balustrades. My silken hands press down on the lids of my eyes.

I live in Bedford Park, in London, in an old black-and-white house that has secret passages. (I'm most scared to be alone and I want most to be alone.) I'm 13 years old, and a child. Rough brown wools rub against my skin, I dream of being warm again, laughing as if I were in a dark, rainy wood.

I dream I see an old wood house on the corner of a town street. A furniture van drives up to the house; two men carry furniture into the house. The house is empty again. I look at the house: in one window an old woman clings to a sash. She says there are ghosts in the house. Opposite the house, when it is black, the young novices of God start screaming.

I kill a duck so I am evil. No one punishes me: my grandfather rewards me and tells the servant to cook the duck for supper. I wiggle my cock at my (grand)mother.

I have to disintegrate my mind to the point my mind is inseparable from the common mind or my "unconscious." By thinking: dreaming, following sexual and other desires, and by inflaming you with sensuous images, we can get rid of the universities, the crowded towns, the bureaucracies. I call up images of myself, or just images. They are "my" images and yet, they extend my knowledge. I usually find out that other people have the same images, and I know we are all connected. Fucking is a religious ceremony. People who have died are still thinking and choosing, for all thoughts and desires are connected and pulsing, in the utter blackness, back and forth. I'm not sure of this.

Images exist, and the causes of, reasons for the images. Sometimes I believe there are no causes or images. Or no images, just the causes: fire, earth, air, water. These four also might be images and hidden: another reason or cause: an endless unknown infinity. I am an old man talking.

If everything is drag, there is no such event as real love or friendship. I am drag too. Other people, dead or alive, are presences: I can sit next to the fire, I cannot enter into it. I want too much to become the people I love: I have too high an idea of friendship and love and suffer each time I fuck or talk to someone. The gods are those who infinitely desire to become other people and so, suffer endlessly. I begin to study myself again, since I have no one else to touch.

Sometimes, when I feel most in child drag, I act shy I can't speak to anyone. I lie down and watch people, open to embrace anyone who sits next to me or talks to or touches me. Usually the people ignore me, and I go home. Only at these strange moments, I call them nymphomaniac moments I feel free; otherwise I'm scared. Hate. Most of my life is hating people or events. I am not happy but am at ease, open only when I'm in drag. In my head I'm always talking to someone (I have few real people to talk to) and when I forget, the two voices go on in my head, I sometimes think one or both of the voices are outside my head, I decide I'm insane.

The dreams and fantasies and desires these events show are growing:

I dream I set out from Sligo, green on green on green, I walk slowly I can't tell if I'm in dream or reality, the thoughts move past me as does the silk outside my eyes, the trees streams are an endless black-and-white silk screen. I can't sleep anymore because I'm so lonely. I'm scared the wood ranger who guards this forest will shoot me. I wake up just as the birds start crying, the small birds, inside and outside of me. Now I long for the country again.

I resolve to work harder and worship my passions. I dream that I walk through the dry forest, branches crackle under my toes; suddenly the ground gives way and I'm walking through a kind of sticky leech-ridden mud. Through endless miles of my blood. Smells. I'm in a nightmare because I have nowhere to go I start crying my uncle says "You have good right to be fatigued" meaning "Who did you fuck?"; I start screaming louder and louder. I'm not explaining why I feel so strongly, why I hate and love, and finally, despite all childhood reasons, I don't know.

K also writes about this and her memory of it is the same as mine:

I'm sitting under an old-fashioned mirror and I'm sitting in another part of the room. An old-fashioned room: brown walls, small, white-lace cloaks. Suddenly I hear a sound as if somebody's throwing a shower of peas at the mirror. Later I see the ground under the trees burning a great light. As I cross the river to a destroyed town, I see the same light moving over a torrent of water. A man walks toward the water and disappears in the water. A small light moves over the Knocknarea slope; in five minutes reaches the summit.

11.

Age 16

In my blue jumper and middy blouse, I'm standing on the corner of 42nd Street and Sixth Avenue, I've just skipped out of my private prison school, noon, and made it down to these initial investigation grounds.

I keep having this dream that I'm in a gang dressed in black everyone's dressed in black; I walk into a huge room it becomes a gym, the only windows are tiny square windows a few feet below the ceiling. I'm alone in the gym, on the polished floor, and I can do anything I want. Suddenly there's a figure sitting in the window in the right-hand corner of the gym; I see a close-up: puffy yellow-white skin blotches distortion the most hideous and evil face possible I scream all the doors to the gym disappear.

Businessmen in gray and brown suits hurry past me; a few look lasciviously into my face. Puke. I see a thin guy, hanging outside a dirty movie house, whose skin looks like it's hanging from his bones. He doesn't notice me. Another guy walks past me wheeling a metal rack with three TV's piled on each other. I see a cheap meat house, hangout for junkies, hookers, etc. I hope, I'm too young to hang out in a bar and I look even younger, walk into it. As I'm getting my cup of brown turd, a voice yells out my name,

"Kid, over here, to your left."

I see two spectral eyes shining out of a white mask; black curling hair falls over the left eye. I recognize Harvey the Bagel.

"Harvey, what . . ."

"Shh, I'm not Harvey anymore, I'm Mommy. You've got to watch your step. How're you kid; I heard you'd come up in the world, your parents making their money back haw haw. You look like you're twelve years old."

My clothes don't mean shit. "I'm older than you." While I'm talking, I pretend that I'm in the jungle: I walk through the stone park, around an iron railing which stops kids from jumping in the river, down some brown soil, to the East River. The garbage-water. A strong rush of water grabs hold of my body, I let my body go to the current, the current bears me down, around one turning, around a second, around a third whirr; at the end a gentler stream bears my exhausted body to a patch of dirt outside a thick jungle. A group of naked women find me, carry me up a path to a clearing which is their home. Tall thin trees shoot out of the bare soil. I learn they are a tribe of young women; a middle-aged woman is their chief. I have one special friend with whom I fuck the main ritual: each woman has to have one operation: a triangle is cut out of her left thigh, then out of her left breast. I shiver in horror. A lobotomy. I want to run away . . .

Mommy's getting pissed that I'm not listening closely to him. "I'll tell you how you can get control of 42nd Street. Listen, Turk. There are two gangs who own 42nd Street: the Mafia, and the Jewish mafia. The Jewish mafia is mainly this one guy, Mart, who owns the peep shows and the dancing girls. The Mafia and he share the sex shows and junk's junk. That's the economics. There're also the cops who are basically paid off by both

Mafias, but who also want their nooky and get it. Like free meals, free snow, free Cadillacs, you know the deal."

"How do you know all this?"

"About a month ago, the regular Mafia offered Mart a deal, a sort of partnership: combine against the cops. Mart thought he'd lose money and didn't take it. So the Mafia's starting an all-out war on him: they're bribing the cops, double what he bribes them, to get him nailed."

"So what's the big schtick? The bum'll get nailed."

"No. There's too much money involved: Mart's given the D.A. too much money. Mart's a cool guy. I've seen him yell in court at a judge who tried to fine him, Mart waved a bunch of hundreds in his hand.

"What's the matter: didn't I bribe you enough?"

"Not here. Not here."

They're not gonna get rid of Mart, but they'll make it hot for him."

"How can you get control of 42nd Street?"

"Plant a lot of bombs, and scare the shit out of the bunch of them. Also separate the men and women. They finally won't be scared, but they'll be tired, and want to get out. They'll give the place to anyone."

Later, I rise from my own bed, open the bedroom door and close it, walk down a small hall, turn left, walk down a long hall, my whole family's asleep, into a kitchen. There's only diet bread, diet margarine, and my wine in the small fridge. I drink a half a glass of wine, quickly, open a lower drawer. I pick up a larger knife, a bread knife, pick it up in my right hand; I leave the kitchen, open the door to my parents' bedroom. As I black out I notice they're both asleep. . . . When I come to, everything's black. I walk over to my mother's bed. My father's no longer snoring. I see two black pools, one on each of the beds. The bread knife's still in my hand, unused.

I walk slowly back, through the blackness, to my room.

> Me, Murderess
> 1947–1964
> A Celebration
> "She learned to love sky blue."

End of the dream.

12.

Age 16

Earlier the same night my sister and I are lying together in bed in the dark green room. My sister thinks my parents are asleep in their bedroom, down the hall from here. Good liberal parents: they don't read too much, but they think Kennedy could have saved the world; they spend a quarter of their money on appearances, put the rest in a bank. A trust fund for me and my sister, paid to each of us on the day of their death. They want the best of everything for us: we should marry rich and get a lot of alimony. My grandmother has bought them a summerhouse in Connecticut, a farm with real chickens and strawberries; they belong to an exclusive beach club, except that it's Jewish. I have as many clothes as I want, as many books, as many boyfriends. Everything money can buy.

"Do you think they're asleep?"

My younger sister looks up at me. She has brown hair, slightly lighter than mine, brown eyes; she's fatter than I am. Depends on me and dislikes me a bit because my mother keeps setting me up to her as an example of goodness and wisdom. Though, to my face, my mother tells me I'm too smart for my own good. Big shit. My sister and I used to fight like suicides: she'd snore, I'd bite through her knees. Now that we're mature (we know about money), we're getting along extremely well.

"You know they're asleep: daddy falls asleep now at 7:30. He's getting drunker and drunker all the time. He couldn't even stand straight after supper. Didn't you hear him whining at mommy saying he doesn't like any of her friends?"

"Do you think he's stealing our money?"

"He hasn't got the guts to do anything illegal. It's mommy and nana (the grandmother): those two are always in cahoots. They see each other every day to play cards."

"How d'you think we can get back our money? They're just a bunch of crooks," I say philosophically.

"We'll have to wait until we're 21. Then hire our own lawyer. I tried to find out from mommy who their lawyer is, but she's sneaky, she wouldn't tell me a goddamned thing."

"Try nana. She's the weaker one."

"Nah, she's too senile or she pretends she's senile: she just starts giving a lecture how I should get better marks at school. Then she tells me she'll take me to the best restaurant in New York for dinner, takes me to Longchamps where I vomit three times."

"Maybe you could find out from daddy."

"He's too stupid to remember. We're going to have to get that money another way."

"Do you want to get married?"

My sister stares at me. "You know my friend Magnesium?"

"The one with the long face and long hair?"

"Yeah, that's the one. She just stayed over here last week. One night last year she took me to this bar, you know, one of those bars where women dance only with women."

"That's weird."

"There were no men in the bar. We walked into the bar, and she kissed some strange women hello, started dancing with one of them. Then I danced with her for about two hours; I felt her lips on my shoulders and on my lips. Her body pressed against mine I felt one of her legs between my legs all the while we were dancing."

I wonder why my sister's telling me this. I don't know what to do.

"Are you a virgin?"

I decide to stop lying. I'm no longer lying. I've learned how to lie too easily and too often from my mother. "No, when I was 13 . . ."

"I'm not a virgin either. I lost mine yesterday, I really hurt; you see, there was this party at Grita's house, you know Grita. Everyone from school was there, including those two whores, Sally and Smelly. David was after me, and so was Stub: I liked both of them, and I felt real happy, I still can't decide which one I should go with. We were all drinking and smoking, you know how it is. Sally and Smelly got in the bathtub and took off their clothes, started yelling "Do it! Do it!" I was scared, you know: that's no way to behave: mommy and daddy totally wouldn't approve. I was sitting on Stub's lap drinking from a can of beer; suddenly I noticed the lights were out and I couldn't see anyone. I heard a lot of moaning and giggling."

"Uh-huh."

"I felt something warm touch the hair between my legs, press, I thought I should cry out because that's the right thing to do, but I didn't want the warmth to stop. Stub, I guess it was Stub, bit and licked my shoulder the two of them started laughing I felt warm shivers go up down my spine. The hand started to mold my cunt it was clay, three fingers slipped around the elastic under the elastic to touch my hair below my hair at a really sensitive area then darted into me. I started to scream I was scared I hurt the fingers moved in me I don't know I felt good my bottom area was growing, turning, something turned in me I wanted something more . . . the fingers slipped out of me, before I could stop, four hands grasped the upper elastic of my pants took them off. I didn't want to see and I wanted to see them come off. I felt free very warm the hands running up down my legs inside my legs made me warmer I wanted to show how good I felt, I reached out my arms I felt a heavy body bear down on me the weight felt terrific like a heavy thick blanket in snow . . .

"When I was 10, I was dating this guy Hammerblunt, remember him, he took me to his apartment, an apartment below his parents' penthouse they owned a building overlooking south Central Park, the first time we had seen each other we had kissed, second time, he touched my breasts, third time he took my clothes off and lay down on my body, pressing against the spot between my legs, continuous wave-explosions blasted through me, I kept holding him back, and not wanting to hold him back; this time we immediately took off all our clothes and lay against each other on this huge darkened white bed, I remember him sitting in a velvet armchair, my sitting on his lap . . .

"I was scared: I was burning like I've never been before I held on to the body suddenly a long hard object I think it was alive jammed up me between my legs I couldn't figure out how it got in, no, I couldn't think I only felt white and yellows, beans burst inside my head I fainted, when I came to I felt the thing traveling up down inside me my nerves exploded first in my intestines then in my stomach and legs then up down my spine I held on to his back kissed the beginning of the back again and again threw my body upwards my cunt upwards to get more the thing in me quivered up and down, and was still.

"I was sitting in Hammerblunt's lap; he placed his mouth on mine; his tongue buried itself in my throat curling uncurling so the waves traveled up down my throat I began to shiver he wrapped two long arms around me drew me into his huge body until I was nothing, he started to whisper to me.

"'Don't be scared; I just want to make you feel good. Tell me if you're too scared and want me to stop.'

"I rubbed my head against his chest, I turned my head and bit the underside of his chin. We started to giggle madly. We kept giggling, he placed his right hand over my cunt, pressed one finger into my cunt, he had never done that before, it hurt, the hurt stopped, three fingers, it hurt, the hurt stopped, the whole hand with the thumb at the edge of my second cunt. We were both giggling madly, two waves, or sheets opening the nerves twisted upward from my cunt, I wanted him to continue . . .

"Do you think I was wrong?" My sister looks at me. "I'm scared I did something I shouldn't have—"

Stupid guilt. I kiss my sister's brown head.

"'Do you want to fuck?'

"'I don't know what you're talking about.'

"Hammerblunt rises from the chair, still holding me, without letting me go, lies face down on the soft bed. As we sink into miles of feather, white air, he takes his cock, places it next to the center of my body. 'You're still dry.' Lightly caresses me with his cock my head whirls I'm not sure anymore what's happening I feel large not strong sensations inside my body above the ends of my legs and in my lips I want them to continue they must be pleasure I want to feel pain no pain a sudden swirl of burning irritation so that I want more starts from my clit up to the middle of my skull, after which I feel nothing. Happy. I fall asleep. I figure out that I've just fucked.

"A week later I split up with Hammerblunt. In spite of our fucking, he doesn't ask me to his school dance at Riversmell, and he has pimples."

I lean over my sister, look at her brown eyes. "We're going on a journey, first to Egypt, home of women who are half animals . . ." I travel my hand lightly over the dark hairs growing out of her stomach. ". . . then to Istanbul, red-and-black land, land of black feathers and gold-and-white-brocade sheets, leathers as soft and thick as your skin, leathers that contain our hatred . . ." My finger finds her clit by its throbbing; I press up and down on it, her body begins to tremble I'm again giving her pleasure I press my finger down harder and harder at the same time I wrap my legs around one of her legs make her leg into a giant cock both our bodies tremble each giant flash of fire inside me makes my fingers move faster I have to go slower: I touch her outer lips thick, rubbing and rubbing until her lower body moves in rhythms with my hands, my fingers, as we meet I let my fingers become feathers against the brown skin between her lips barely against now, against her clit my fingers move faster and faster I forget about her. A long swirl of irritation a burning nerve bursts from my clit. "Have you gone enough; are you there?" My sister kisses my lips, and nods. "Go to sleep sweet."

That night my sister and I, frightened out of our wits, split the city. My sister disappeared; I went to the coast, changed my name to Rip-off Red, started to starve. As far as I know, the police never searched for my sister and me: in New York they only care about pot-heads and political kids. I never saw anyone I knew in my childhood, again.

snow petals hang from sapphires a summer's day

Part Three

13. May 3

"Do you want to be with me?"

I walk away from Peter Peter, part of me doesn't want to walk away, down through the rows of white seats an outdoor auditorium, night, across the dirt center I don't walk through the dirt to where a woman's sitting. I walk into the crowded theater by myself I'm an outcast. I'm an outcast. On my left a small group of women talk to each other. Is this true? A woman with white skin brown hair a few inches taller than me talks to me; we put our arms around each other's shoulders. She wears red. A thin yellow-haired woman walks up to me: we laugh in greeting. I walk away with the thin brown-haired woman, and. sit down next to her, now I'm officially a lesbian, across the ring from Peter Peter.

Later Peter Peter, the woman, and I walk through dark green leaves into a wood house. The house is strange, gray wood, many levels of roofs. An old woman with a silver platter in her hand: "Hello. Please sit down." Sit down on red velvet chairs around a wood dining-room table, brocaded walls, shut windows look into the night. Three women live in this house. I find out the women are vampires: they induce me and Peter Peter to wrap ourselves into the walls of the house. Peter Peter somehow dies. One of the women entraps me—I become an underdone chicken yellow skin on yellow flesh on the silver platter, through my legs at the curve of my neck flows yellow-red blood.

The story of the desperate attempt to which we have committed ourselves begins. My lover and I stand in a high off-white Spanish room, thousands of low arches. To my right, an arched doorway. A woman walks into the room; I pull out my gun, brandish it; a black dog with long knotted fur wallops over to me, I play with him, he's going to shit, move him. I'm sitting inside a bathroom a few inches up from the floor of the Spanish room, off-white walls, I'm trying to shit; various people passing by ask me if I'm O.K. All my relatives. Finish shitting, the muscles around the hole expand contract partly at will, feel good, turn to my right: I see a blonde woman: my mother. All my relatives tell her, "We don't love you." I sit separate from these people, behind and to the right of them, on the floor. My mother walks over to me, past my pretend father I become my pretend father, standing behind me to my right. My mother says, "You're the only one I trust." I realize she's mentally weak. On the floor near the back right-hand corner of the room a flawless natural 6-carat ruby, redder than the blood of owls, lies, touching nothing.

"Listen, Peter Peter," I'm announcing, "this is what's going to happen:

"Tonight we're going to finally find out about this Spitz guy. The whole works. You're going to follow him at the usual 10:00 P.M. to this Irish Saloon joint, where we always lose him, just to be sure he doesn't pull any funny stuff, go somewhere else. Not that I think he will. At 10:00 P.M. I'll be at the Irish Saloon, casing the joint, seeing what happens there before the old guy makes his appearance. On second thought, maybe I'll go earlier, become pals with the customers. Mm-mmm."

Peter Peter starts to glower. He looks gorgeous in his new black rimless glasses.

"This is the way we'll succeed. So when schnookums enters this Irish Saloon, I'll immediately know where he goes, and you can follow me to see I don't get killed or mutilated. Tomorrow night we'll see Loulou, Dicky Dick, and Julie, tell them the results. If they're not the culprits."

What is the nature of reality?

I'm scared I'm frightened to death I'm petrified there's a man after me a thick translucent white jellyfish no eyes I'm walking down a wide street I hear yells screams I start to run a gang's behind me one hatchet passes me another hatchet glances into my right calf falls to the cement I run faster faster the men run faster.

I'm tough I can do anything I wear black leather bands around my wrists around my ankles no other clothes a thick bicycle chain around my neck if I have to I can sleep with anyone a man a jellyfish no compunctions I just can't stand to talk to them I have no morals I can rob without being caught pretend I'm sweet and innocent in pink organdy pretend I know everything about sex I won't let anything disturb you harm you my tailored black suit and silk stockings tan Gucci scarf with sailors from all over the world. I know everything.

I destroy I burn college buildings and laugh I destroy college professors cops who think they can stick their noses into my business quickly learn better the flames are beautiful I tear up pictures of Nixon teach younger lovers to make Molotov cocktails.

I don't want anyone to touch me stick thin finger knives into my brain and destroy my brain bother me pretend to like me then hit me over the head lure me into revealing myself and opening myself then turn away "goodbye your cunt's too wet."

Most people are stupid boring too much fire inflammations result I'd rather be alone shut the door shut the bedroom door I live in furs under a black bear blanket I swathe myself in velvets.

I love being severe and elegant I wear only scarves around my body I know the special places in New York: the massage parlors for women, the hundred-dollar wines I can stick my tongue out at the top pleasures no one can possibly kill me.

I don' t care if I'm alone I want a permanent and a temporary lover-friend I don't want to know anyone else no one else exists I want to leave my town house on 61st Street between Second and Third once a week enter into a room in which there are thousands of people I want to meet love as much as possible go home to drink by myself I'm extremely shy I don't fuck as much as I want.

6:00 P.M. Already dark.

I put my arms around Tough Tits, an older Indian woman, she responds puts her arms around me Peter Peter and another thin blonde woman are in the room with us my left hand moves to the center of her back, presses her back toward my body, we hold each other closer and closer. I want to go to the beach; I leave the small wood house; walk down a path in between small boulders to a pool set in the odd-shaped rocks. Most of the pool is shallow, in one part near the center my body can sink into the cool water. Huge sun overhead. Many women crowd the pool, too many bodies, I can't swim. I walk back up the steep path to the wood house; there's a beach below the level of the rocks of the pool. Can I get to the beach? Two women passing by me tell me to walk south a few blocks, then I'll find a dirt path down through the cliffs to the ocean. I dream of swimming a black calm ocean under a black sky. Drunk. I tell the older woman about the path to the ocean. She and the blonde woman are walking north to a larger house. Do I want to travel with her, the blonde woman, both of them?

I find a closer sand path, through the burning cliffs, hot sun, to the sand and the ocean running cold without end to the north, south, and west.

Should I go to the Irish Saloon as a man or a woman? I contemplate wearing my mod Mad. Ave. disguise: brown curly mustache slightly lighter than my hair, light makeup on cheeks to give the appearance of roughness, green corduroy pants and vest, a tie with large black designs. Think I'm feeling fem tonight. Besides, Spitz's father is a man; I'll have to persuade the men at the bar, probably, not the women, who know something to tell me what they know. In this case, better be female.

I quickly put on a blue crepe forties' dress, cut with long legs, wide hips, a slit that runs up to my cunt two inches away from my cunt, purple suede shoes with thin flicker knives concealed in the heels, huge rubber heels that help me take the heights and jumps, invisible ankle supports, my silver ankh ring, and a long velvet velvet-lined cape. Peter Peter's in the bathroom shitting and smelling up the place. Ha ha. He'll have to leave soon too. I fasten the diamond clasps of the cape; walk out the door.

Only 6:33 P.M.; I have to be at the Irish Saloon by 8:30 or 9:30. Plenty of time to get all the information I need. Black and purple New York streets. As I'm pretending I'm transforming into a New York mugger I've got my hands on my stick, I'm scanning the street for unescorted rich women, lonely filthy alleys to which I can drag the women, I notice a man, no, a boy, dark hair, dark eyes, a few inches taller than me, walking beside me. I walk faster; the boy walks faster.

"Can I help you?"

I don't answer; slow down, suddenly walk faster, slow down again. He hangs on like a lonely cat. I want to get rid of him because I'm scared, but he' s awfully cute.

"What's your name?"

"Rip-off."

"Can I go out with you?"

No answer. We walk up Fifth Avenue past areas of light, a sudden garden, a bored cop. No junkies around. Rubies and sapphires and emeralds and diamonds. The sky, wherever I can catch a glimpse of it, *when I stop being scared long enough to look straight over my head,* is purple-gray-blue.

I'm more scared than interested. I see Doubleday's ahead; I start walking faster.

"Where are you going?"

I suddenly reach a bookstore. Safety. The boy follows.

"I'd like to take you home to meet my parents." He's Mexican, wearing a gray, cheapy suit, carries a slim black briefcase. I ignore him, walk to the poetry books, paper ones, the middle section of the store. As I'm looking at the books, I feel a hand on my cheek, the hand gently turns my head around, soft lips very lightly touch my lips. I feel like I'm falling asleep in a huge thick bed.

"Do you want to fuck me?"

"No. I want to take you home with me, to meet my parents."

His huge hands go around my head, help me hold up the heavy weight of the head, his lips descend on me, enter me. In my mouth they touch my cheeks, my warm tongue, hold my tongue as it searches, find his tongue, wrap around each other, lightly, away, hold each other again with desire. I put my arms around his shoulders, feel the beginning weight of his body.

"Tell me that you want to fuck me. I can understand you then."

"I would like to introduce you to my parents. You are very nice and beautiful."

I'm in a small alley filled with cardboard boxes, garbage, the boy is standing over me, one of his hands on my stomach, gently presses and strokes. I allow him to fuck me, although I know if he fucks me, he will then be able to murder me. My body leans flat against a concrete wall, the upper half of the body leaning to the right; my body snaps into two pieces.

My hand takes one of his hands; we walk out of the store. 7:00 P.M.

"Where do you want to go?"

We race down 56th Street, past Madison, past Park, past Lexington, past Third Avenue. Sometimes we pass by a few robots. Between two staircases to brownstones, there's a staircase going downward, below the brown street. We see no lights in the windows of the lower house. The boy races down the steps, dragging me with him, back into the black shadows of the building. His two hands grasp my shoulders, wrapped in the black velvet cape, sets me against the hard stone.

"I love you."

He leans his body against mine, hard, I can feel the beginning of his limbs, the bulge of his stomach, as he can feel me, my breasts and my legs O his hands rip under the dress at the slit rub against my bulging stomach then outline the creases that run above my thighs from my cunt out to my sides the hand brushes slightly over the hairs above the sides of my cunt and the insides of my legs his fingers stroke the moist skin between the top of the legs and the cunt lips.

"I want to fuck, now."

I lie down on the concrete, on the velvet lining on the cape, watch the boy undo his belt, then the waist of his pants, I see thin muscles curl around his legs, a round large ass, good, his cock's huge is it too big? I don't want to have to ignore the pain he moves slower than me forces me to feel the increasing tensing then relaxing of my muscles, the small white lights that shoot to the top of my skull, explode, I don't want to let go of the heat I let go underneath or inside the heat gathers rises to the front of my body. He quickly falls on top of me I feel heavy weight I try to lift into it, into him, as I slowly raise my cunt, now the center of my body, my right hand touches his cock, long and thin, I don't want him to hurt me, I place his head between my lips. I raise up fear: am I dry am I hot? I don' t know anything anymore. Soft lips come down on mine and a tongue descends nerves rasp burn around my cheeks in swirls to the inside the centers of my nipples I rub my breasts against him as hard as I can. Again his tongue descends, his unclean water mixes with mine, I want to hold him and rock him, put my winding arms around and around his body and roll around inside and outside as the heat finally gathers again and again his slippery tongue descends I try to hold on tense my muscles I'm beginning to dream.

"What's your name?"

"Manuel."

His finger descends, enters the inside of my ass, my whole body tenses, explodes, his fingers begin to move around, tiny circles which widen and widen, I come again and again, flames rush to the edges of my skins, explode, rush outward at the edge of real pain the finger moves out of the asshole I become still.

We start moving against each other slowly faster and faster my skin becomes mlllions of tiny diamonds separating from each other I feel Manuel become me rush me into violent explosions I begin to dream I pound my thighs and belly against harder and harder the skin between my ass and cunt vibrates sending stronger vibrations up through my cunt his skin then straight to my inflamed clit. A black cat comes over to me, rubs against me.

For a moment I hold Manuel's black curly head in my arms. We softly murmur.

"What do you know about Sally Spitz's murder?"

"Nothing yet. I'm going to find out tonight about her father's connection to the Irish Saloon." I murmur back. "Is her murder connected to her father's strange behavior?"

Suddenly I'm very frightened. I jump up, grab my cape, race down 56th Street to First Avenue. I'm too confused to think straight. Above me, the New York sky is now black. I look behind me, but I don't see Manuel.

First Avenue, 55th Street. What's Manuel's connection to Spitz's murder? Is he her murderer, responsible for her murder, a jealous boyfriend, a frightened boyfriend? Behind the huge terrifying New York buildings there's some memory. I try not to remember. A car stops suddenly, gnashes its brakes. At the airport:

the guy who was talking to Spitz. Am I sure? Is my memory faulty? I don't like the idea of Spitz having boyfriends. O.K. Manuel wasn't her boyfriend. Shows you where emotion gets you. I decide Manuel's connected in some way or ways to the father' s nightly disappearings, probably also Spitz's murder. Manuel knows too much; he was deliberately following me: he knew Spitz.

I can barely see the line between the now-black buildings and the black sky except where an occasional streetlight throws out weird shadows. I decide: I'll trap Manuel tonight, keep to my plan of following Spitz's father from the Irish Saloon. I draw my cape around my shoulders to keep me warm and hide me. Like a cat burglar, I sneak from corner to corner, walking against the walls of the buildings in the endless shadows. No one notices me. A cop car passes by me; both cops probably drunk like everyone else. In the sky I see small crystal glasses containing red and violet liqueurs, dull brown liqueurs, jewels I can pour down my throat. I rub my hand against my soft skin.

52nd Street. A cop stands on the opposite corner, talks to himself. I hope he doesn't think I'm a burglar. Too rich a neighborhood for the cops to bother the people, and, besides, this is New York. The buildings are becoming hideous gray and brown monsters who are one day going to stand up, trample down all humans with their golden flat feet. The days of revolution. I sneak along in the shadows I'm invisible and I see no one. I hear no thief's footsteps, Spitz's father doesn't yet appear, across the dangerous street, past a poodle peeing against a fire hydrant: three brown steps leading to a wood door. I look at myself in a window mirror: 8:59 P.M.

And again I walk over to the luxurious bar, throw my cape behind me a mysterious romantic whirl of black. Get them to notice me. In the red lights my green eyes shine like a cat's. I'm haughty, look down on the populace from immeasurable heights. I sight a group of high-class businessmen at the bar, English well-cut suits, feminine faces, one other man at the bar, thin, almost no hair on his head, a brown beard. Probably a playwright. He starts to mumble to himself. I slowly descend, allow my soft ass to rub against the seat of a bar stool.

"A Chivas Regal please. Straight."

Nobody sits down next to me. Nobody tries to talk to me. Black night. The bartender doesn't talk to anyone either, just stands, stares at his fascinating hallucinations.

After about fifteen minutes, a man in a gray suit sits down next to me. Different shades of gray hair swirl around his skull.

"Do you need a job?"

I stare at him in disbelief.

"I'm leaving for Australia in two days and I need to take a woman with me, a secretary, who could train the women in Australia to be secretaries. You have to start with women over here; they don't train them right in Australia. I used to own greyhounds but I sold them all, put my money into Yam-Ham stocks. I'll start Yam-Ham over in Australia. You can't bring American money to Australia: the way the value of the American dollar's declined, I'd lose a fortune. I've got a regular factory over there, a bloody castle."

"What the fuck are you talking about?"

"I'd start you at 25,000 dollars a year. You'd see China, India; you'd travel like you've never dreamed. You'd make a half a million, I could promise you a million dollars inside of ten years. But if you're planning on getting married—"

"I'm sorry. I'm not interested."

"If you'd like to come up to my hotel room, we could have some coffee: discuss matters further."

"I don't want to go to your hotel room."

Another man sits next to me, asks if I'll sleep with him. No. No no no. I become scared of what will happen when Spitz's father arrives, I can't talk to anyone: I'm deaf dumb and blind.

14. May 3

On the moon there are no cities no destruction by human beings, just miles of flourishing vegetation, black rocks, a swirling black sky. I'm no longer scared to fuck with talk to anyone, whether I want to or not.

Spitz's father walks into the bar. Alone. Peter Peter must be close behind. I'm standing toward the back of the bar, behind a pillar. I gather my cloak around me.

The old vegetable seems to see nothing. He quickly walks past the bar, seems to murmur something to the bartender. He walks past the bar into a corridor. I wait a second, follow. I look into the dark corridor, ahead of me see a door open and close. No sign of Peter Peter. The bartender's watching me closely. Just as I dart into the corridor, he yells something behind me. I don't listen. I see the outline of a door beyond the male and female bathrooms. Footsteps behind me. The bartender. I open the door, rush up narrow steps gray light another door I open it: a room dazzling with thousands of mirrors, beneath my foot ivory-gold carpet.

"Can I help you?"

I swirl around, see a young female at a desk. "Huh? What is this joint?"

"This is an exclusive massage parlor: Monsieur Hawk, Ltd. We don't usually cater to women, but if you can tell me who recommended our luxurious services to you, I would be glad to be of assistance to you."

I murmur an apology and rush down the stairs. No need to lose status. Another apology to the bartender; he makes some attempt to detain me. I see Peter Peter, grab his arm, rush out into the dark street.

"Peter Peter it's a fucking massage parlor: Spitz's father goes to a massage parlor; big shit, they're probably rooking him for his money."

Peter Peter thinks quick. "So Spitz was killed by the massage parlor people . . ."

"Monsieur Hawk, Ltd."

" . . . for being interested in her father's nightly escapades? No. More likely the usual nut murdered her."

"More likely the usual nut murdered her."

Part Four

SONG OF THE ICEBOATS
MOON PEOPLE
15. May 3

Peter Peter and I continue to walk that night down the filthy garbage streets of the jungle, our hands clasped. We pass packs of wild dogs howling at our heels, yipping into the black air, there are no more people, open garbage cans past open garbage cans, strange lights peering into our eyes. Tall buildings like giant dogs move behind the clouds. We carry police whistles in our mouths, spit drools from our lips, we whimper to fit your vision of lunatics escaped from Bellevue so you won't mug us. We hide behind each car, race to the back of another car, to the back of another car. Too hard work. We're two people, alone, walking great distances.

"I need a drink, I'm dying, I need snails with a lot of garlic sauce, a Lafitte-Rothschild '01."

"Haw. Haw. I was almost just killed," I sagely reply.

"I need venison soaked in mace and port, covered with huge chunks of creamery butter, followed by a ton of Beluga, chopped ducks' eggs, Altadena sour cream. And white chocolate.

"I want it right now."

"Listen. This city's about to collapse. The planet-country-empires are destroying New York (us): they're sending Z-bombs to attack our intestines and hearts, heart attacks; they're causing the huge pathways of the city like giant snakes to turn on themselves, make people go crazy on the streets, make people have to take increasing dosages of speed-junk, make people murder, sexually assault."

"It's just some guys have too much money."

51st Street. 52nd Street. 53rd Street. 54th Street. First Avenue. Second Avenue. I repeat these names a sacred litany my first truest love no matter how fast you're, like Europe did, dying, how you're bumbling into deserted streets and bumble, houses containing broken arms and legs.

"Peter Peter, don't cry. We don't have to leave here. We don't ever have to return to San Diego. We'll just travel around and around, do whatever we want, until we die."

"You're not practical." He puts his hand on his hip, smiles, looks around in the murky air. I think I see a faint glimpse of the moon, but can't tell. Still trembling from the encounter in the massage parlor, like when I once took a trick when I was broke and starving in San Diego in the early days. Not really a trick: a photographer, sort of a friend, was going to do a free portfolio of me for me, we were smoking, would I do some nude shots for him for playing cards? O by the way, he needed to shoot his own cock in the photo. Fifty dollars for an hour's work. Big shit. The black sky swirls into my face.

A hand grabs my hand, drags me across the thin street, my feet shuffling, into a tiny dark doorway. I look up: Louie's Joint. The hand opens the door, drags me into a tiny bar, one line of chairs between a bar and wood wall, one or two tables in the back. We shift past the chairs to the back, seat ourselves at the only unoccupied table. I can see the other table to the right and back of me, a small mirror, partly covered with dust, on the back wall. Some kind of Muzak manages to reach my ears.

"Listen, Rip-off," Peter Peter murmurs.

"Two straight whiskeys please."

"We've got to stop this detective business. You're no longer a detective, that's all there is to it. It's too dangerous here. We'll see Loulou and Julie tomorrow night, tell them the crooks, or the crooks and the murderers, Monsieur Hawk, Ltd., whoever that is: we'll never see anyone again. If you keep investigating, you're going to get yourself killed. As broke and crazy as you are. You can decide to be something else, something safer, like a gangster, or a scuba diver, or a politician. You're just going to stop."

"Are you trying to tell me what to do?" He begins to cower. Rightfully. Peter Peter always knows how to get around me. "We've had this stupid conversation before," I continue. "In New York the chances are always better than 50 percent that you and I will get mugged, raped, and run over by a fed-up taxi driver. As if some real criminal had a chance to hurt us. At the beginning of this investigation," I take another sip of whiskey, "I vowed and dedicated myself to finding the murderer of my love. That is a sacred dedication."

Peter Peter understands.

"Anyway the massage parlor's probably the culprit. Our task is successfully finished."

"I don't know," Peter Peter murmurs, "those massage parlors, poor and plush, rake in the money without doing anything wrong. They might get a guy hooked, you know, supplying whatever stuff the guy needs that either he can't get elsewhere or that he can't get elsewhere without a lot of hassle, but they're not going to rip off some guy's relative or friend 'cause that person's in the know about the massage parlor."

"Pig," I murmur.

"Moreover you know Loulou and Julie are pretty hip. I wonder what this father needs that he has to pay for. And pay a lot; it almost looks like blackmail. We ought to investigate further only," the tone of his voice changes, "we're drawing out. Blackmail's too dirty for you to get involved in. Too dangerous."

"I'll do what I want, sweetheart, and remember that." I'm wearing my Mae West voice. I think hard about the problem at hand. "No, it's not blackmail: a place that posh by the U.N. wouldn't bother to resort to blackmail. Spitz's father is the bourgeois type: he wants to fuck, or whatever he does to get off, probably fuck, though you never know about these types, but he needs to do it in secret, not with his pure wife; he even needs to pay money. He wields the power behind closed doors."

"He probably just likes a dame who works there who's rooking him blind. People act crazy when they decide they're in love. It doesn't all mean something."

"I don't agree." We're about to have another of those stupid arguments in which we never know what we're arguing about, and we actually agree with each other. I look around the smoky bar, at the decaying wood walls, a yellow sign:

> WOMEN AND CHILDREN
> ARE ALLOWED IN THIS BAR
> ONLY IF THEY ARE SILENT

At the bar a woman's screaming at her husband, telling him that she earns all the money and does all the cooking, and there's never enough liquor to drink.

"Peter Peter, tell me again about your strange childhood. I love you so much."

"I have a vision," says Peter Peter. "Women and men, women-men and men-women parade around an open field. Large birds huge red and purple feathers mixed with black fur land start walking around us. I put my arm around one of the long necks of the birds. If I wanted to, I could change the scene. Around the field is an endless beach and beyond the beach, an ocean. The whole beach is lit by the phosphorescence of the waves. On the black sand, thousands of tiny fish, brought in by the huge waves, leap over each other, fuck, lay eggs, are left stranded on the sands. Silver on silver.

"I have a dream, a picture and a hope of a better world. A city in which people want to stay alive, a city full of screaming howling insane people, people who refuse to be robotized react at the slightest rejection. People who shit in the streets who infiltrate every system which exists. People who refuse to obey themselves or anyone else, who refuse to plan future systems to which they'll have to bend. People who make sunlight, then proceed to make silver moons gleaming through the thin black glass of buildings, copper reflecting faces on copper back to the forty stories of copper rising past the wings of airplanes."

"I think it's time to go." I manage to rise out of my chair, peer through the opaque smoke for my black cape. A thin figure, seated at the bar, looks vaguely familiar. I try to clear the smoke around me, look; I see black curly hair, a slim body in a gray business suit. I begin to get scared again.

"What's the matter?"

I don't want to tell Peter Peter anything.

"That guy over there; the one seated on the second stool to the right: I think he's connected with Spitz's murder."

"How do you know that? I've never seen him before."

"Trust me."

I look at Manuel out of the corner of my eye. He turns his head, quickly looks at us, turns his head back to normal. He's not here by accident. Why did he ask me those questions about Spitz? He must have followed me to the massage parlor, then here. I'm scared of him I'm scared I fucked him.

"We can't leave the bar right now."

I start to tell Peter Peter about my childhood, how I lied and lied and lied. Any conversation that seems casual and wastes time.

After what seems hours Manuel rises up, walks into the smog toward the door. He doesn't turn his head again to look at us. I tell Peter Peter we can go.

We walk slowly past the empty bar stools into the New York streets. I look around carefully, no sign of anyone. As we walk up to Third Avenue, I listen closely between the beats of our footsteps, I hear no other footsteps. I begin for the first time tonight to feel safe.

Hawks, or gulls, pass over our heads, screaming loudly. We walk past huge piles of dog shit, concrete stairways jutting into the thin streets, pieces of red and green glass reflect the lights of street lamps. Peter Peter's shadow hovers over mine. Mad dogs race down the black streets; in the distance I see birds with endless pointed beaks attack the top of a building; they drive their beaks against the building, brush their metal wings against the corners of the building, I see the single building slowly crumbling to the ground.

As Peter Peter and I turn the corner to reach our hotel, a long thin knife whistles past me, an inch in front of my body.

Nothing else happens to us.

All the people I know are dead people. Spitz's father, Loulou, Julie. I haven't seen or talked to anyone in years, no matter how often I make love.

16. May 4

J'm lying again in Loulou's arms, looking up at her thin, elegant face. She manages to smile at me. I'm going crazy: I haven't slept with a woman in 48 hours. I have dreams upon dreams of sleeping with strange women, women who look like long lanky dogs, women who tease me until I fall madly in love with them and then run away. I wake up, go back to sleep, finding no relief anywhere. I think too much about sex, fantasize embroider I'm slowly becoming a sex maniac; taking myself away from the pain of my ulcer, I wrap myself in fantasies and realities that resemble nothing except the coldest snow. Throwing white cloth over a dead body. Finally I think that coming's unimportant, an activity that's secondary, for when I finish being a detective. I wrap myself in silk; I surreptitiously slide my hand down my tender belly across the rise into my thick hairs.

I raise my head toward Loulou's head until my lips for some reason trembling brush against her thin chin. As she lowers her chin, I quickly thrust my face between her chin and shoulder, with my sharp teeth and tongue nibble at tease brush lick bite the muscle that runs down her neck an inch below her right ear, two inches below her right cheek, three inches under her chin around and around until I reach the hollow at her left shoulder at the end of the neck. I lightly skim her her skin touch her skin I want shivers to start running up down her back I want her body the muscles at the inside of her thighs to ache with need.

Suddenly her hand throws up my chin she leaps over me buries her teeth around a downward muscle of my neck. Bites hard. She lifts her hands bears them down her long nails into the skin of my shoulders and breasts not cutting the skin causing long red marks to appear. Her hands slide down my body: longer red marks following the curves of my muscles. Her nails curve into the sides of my cunt, lightly graze my flesh.

By now we're breathing hard, sweat drips from under our armpits and the insides of our legs, she breathes into my ear, then twists her thin tongue like an animal's into its center, causing me to shudder, grow scared, she rubs her body against me, begins to murmur my desire strangeness while she continues to lick my ear, to bite my soft lobe.

Like a series of separate snowflakes.

The nerves within my inner body my legs and cunt begin to burn rise like yeast: her hand curls down my thigh around the upper leg to its inside to the heavy thick flesh her hand inch by inch brushes up to the red lips the large and salty lips she runs a finger around the edge of the opening too high toward the clit I shudder, down again scratching lightly pulling lightly at the hairs around and around my clit begins slowly to pulse around and around; I'm a forest huge flakes of snow falling catch on the thick black branches hang there on the fur of wolves on the rivers covered by layer on layer on layer of ice wild dogs with long black hairs who can howl like wolves chase after the man-eating wolves. My nerves are trembling, rising and falling, her hand travels in faster and faster circles, until I can hardly bear my desire one finger starts to move inward touch my clit then back around and around my clit begins to throb, she touches it again.

"Loulou, wait. I have to tell you . . ."

"Later."

Again her finger, one finger, begins to trace the avenues of my lips and insides, now in elusive spirals, strange figure eights,

I begin to thrust my hips forward, our breathings harshen, her thumb juts into my cunt like a pussycat's cock the best cock her finger lies on top of my clit press. Press.

As my clit swells my legs begin to tense, I relax enough to begin: and my consciousness and blood drain into my sex, I press myself against her fingers, she swirls faster and faster into me, her fingers pluck with abandon at my clit, I press even harder suddenly she reverses herself throws herself on top of me I'm stunned I adore gangsters and criminals her tongue darts into my vagina around the vagina's edge throwing my orgasm back and open my mouth hits her wet cunt hard faster tongue curls around tongue builds wild Arabian structures horses whose body at the slightest touch quivers who are more sensitive than mother-of-pearl. As my orgasm starts deep in me, I thrust my tongue deep as I can into her, she presses her tongue against my clit, harder and harder. I'm paralyzed I'm pure fire white blast against black wood I phosphoresce and fall. I thrust my tongue even farther into Loulou move it around and around as I feel the soft layers of her walls the mazes of space and flesh layers of flesh on flesh I'm beginning to come again I can feel Loulou's wet body I can feel her cunt muscles open squeeze I can feel her blood pour into my face a tree grows in my head explodes a stupid romantic beast gold diamonds my clit shudders, sends white fluid, vibrating, out of it.

I want each orgasm I have to be the final infinite orgasm; I want to be able to find some kind of rest. As a man or a woman. I want the sex to be rich and incredible. Phooey. Loulou's beginning to bore me, she's too rich and elegant. She'll never have enough guts to get away, to love anyone but herself; she's always looking in a mirror. She's unable to talk about anything but herself, and yet I'm scared of her, I feel like I have to show off around her. I can't joke with her like I do with the few people I can relax around. She fascinates me.

"Loulou, we've got to go into the library and join the men. I don't like fucking up like this when it's not necessary."

The library has ivory-gold walls, thousands of Persian rugs, and no real furniture. Weird in its own way. Peter Peter and Julie sit against a white wall, giggling.

"Come and sit by us, darlings. Peter Peter's absolutely wonderful. You should have introduced him . . ."

"Listen Julie. Loulou. This is serious. Last night Peter Peter and I succeeded in following Mr. Spitz."

"Lacky."

"Oh yeah. Listen. We had already followed Mr. Spitz, Lacky, to this Irish Saloon on First and 51st Street. This time we found out that he goes through the Irish Saloon, through a door in the back to a semiprivate massage joint, Monsieur Hawk, Ltd. Very suave: I saw the joint myself. Ha ha. He probably gives them checks made out for cash so you wouldn't find out. Not that I think you'd care. I didn't find out anything else about the place, but if you want me to I will. If you want, ha ha, I'll give you a written report. Anything for a friend, though I hate using the language."

"But that's completely nuts. Listen," Loulou explodes, "to me. When I met Lacky I was in 11th grade, in high school, and he was in 12th grade. We both went to private unisex schools. Even then he acted stupid, but he was in my crowd because he was dissolute enough. All we did was fuck and insult each other.

"I liked Lacky because he was the only boy who didn't tell me that I took off my clothes because I wanted to become pregnant. My parents kept me imprisoned in their house, and would only let me out with a boy they knew was rich. Boys were supposed to fuck married women and girls were supposed to be dead. One evening, when my parents were living in their summerhouse on the South Shore of Long Island, I went with Lacky to this awful dance somewhere or other. My parents had given me permission to spend a night at my girlfriend's Hymen Hymen's house in the city. I was drunk, stoned vomiting drunk. I dragged Lacky to my parents' deserted city house, bribed the elevator man to let us in, and threw Lacky on my parents' bed. I threw a sheet over him.

"Lacky, as usual, was terrible, and I was too drunk to do anything. The ceilings of the room kept becoming the walls of a Buddhist temple: I was running back and forth with huge lions.

"I was scared because I knew I shouldn't be alone with a guy, but I also hated, still violently hate, anyone who denies me my pleasures. This fear made me more desperately want to fuck. Lacky lay his huge body on top of mine, his clothes half-on half-off, and started pummelling me. I felt his thick tongue brush the edge of my nipple, my skin felt endlessly thick and soft, he gathered the whole small breast in his mouth and started to suck and suck as a white flame shot to the top of my head and clit. Fur started growing thick over my body. I gathered his head to me, desperate, and fell asleep.

"A door bangs; huge footsteps come down the hall. 'Lacky,' I shake him, 'get the fuck out of here.'

"'What is going on here, and who are you sir?' My father stands over me, screaming. 'I want to talk to you Loulou.'

"I tell Lacky to run, throw some clothes on, go into the kitchen. My father promises me he won't tell my mother. 'Just tell me everything that happened.'

"'Nothing happened, daddy.'

"'What happened?'

"'But daddy, really, *nothing* happened.'

"'Tell me what happened,' he shrieks, 'tell me what happened!'

"Nothing had happened. Lacky is impotent, and would never go to a massage parlor and spend that kind of money for sexual reasons. You'll have to find another explanation, Rip-off."

Waves of terror overwhelm me. I don't know where I'm going or what I'm doing.

"Loulou. Julie. Do you have any idea why Lacky goes every night to this massage parlor?"

"No."

"And we still don't know who killed Sally."

The ocean starts to roll its black waves over me. Mud rises up, swirls over my head. I'm about to be rolled against the harsh sand, to have white spume gather in my mouth, nostrils, ears.

"O.K. Tomorrow I'll go to Monsieur Hawk, Ltd. and get a massage. I need it." I sigh. "I'll find out their cover, how they're taking your husband, even if I have to bomb New York."

I won't be doing anything new.

"Just find out," Loulou orders, "who killed Sally."

Who am I? Why am I a detective?

I don't sleep well at night when I wake up at 7:00 in the morning I can't stand to be touching anyone I have to move around from bed to bed not possible in a hotel room.

I don't like when other people are nervous I don't like green green walls green and purple birds when I fuck Peter Peter I have to tell myself he's Peter Peter I can let myself fuck him I love to fuck strangers I'm not sure if I know how to tell the truth.

I'm supposed to be telling the truth here: I don't like to talk to anyone I hide myself I walk ten feet above the street I like to wear velvet pants huge capes jewels running through my hair silver in the inside of my skin I don't like people who talk about "the elite" I don't fuck people with whom I'm close friends I don't see as many people as I should.

That night Peter Peter Julie Loulou and I all drunk sleep together, at least in the same room. I don't remember who does what. I don' t remember anything anymore, except that I'm hungry and even hornier. I don't see Julie or Loulou Dicky Dick again.

17. May 5

T HE RETREAT FROM EVERYTHING: I'm waking up with a crumbling taste in my mouth and white crust in my eyes. I feel like I've got a stomach-load of vomit; a hammer's hitting my skull every three minutes. Do I ever want to fuck again? Peter Peter's got his baby-blue eyes open. Otherwise everyone's dead. I wink at Peter Peter, grab my black jacket, black shirt, black pants, running tiptoe toward the bedroom door. Fly down the carpeted stairs, open the front door, the building hall. Peter Peter follows close behind me.

"Whew. Thought we'd never make it. I feel lousy. What time is it?"

Peter Peter looks like an overgrown baby. I see the new newspaper headlines:

NIXON MASSACRES CHILE

CHILD MURDERS MOTHER: CHILD JUDGED OBVIOUSLY INSANE

REAGAN TAKES AWAY ALL FOOD FROM POOR

I think of which buildings I'd like to explode. Peter Peter in his black monk's cape climbs onto a low window ledge, starts walking up 57th Street by walking from ledge to hydrant, above building canopies, sleepy angry doormen, down to the next ledge. I stumble down the white street, gasping for water, better for a drink: I'm lost in the Alaskan snows, ten days day after day, a day ago my dogs ran off with my sled, only ten more miles to the nearest post, ten more miles for my aching back and legs. A dog runs past me and begins to howl; then slowly moves away.

Peter Peter jumps from the final building ledge onto the southeast corner of Second and 57th. I wildly applaud. I make my final decision:

"Peter Peter I can't stand lying, I have to confess to you. That evil man, Manuel, we saw in the bar the night before last." Peter Peter looks confused. My tongue keeps flopping all over the place. "The bar we went to late at night, after we found out about the massage parlor, right. In the bar I saw a slim guy with dark hair, gray business suit, he kept watching us secretly, then left, yeah: that's Manuel. I think he threw the knife at me."

"So what."

I find it hard for me to continue. "When I was walking to the Irish Saloon, earlier that same night, a guy tried to pick me up, the usual stuff, I squelched him; another guy started to walk by my side. I hurried up, slowed down, stopped, turned fast corners: no help. In a bookstore he started to kiss me, thick warm lips down on my lips. He told me he wanted to take me home with him to meet his parents."

"What else happened?"

"I've never been seduced before. I dragged him to a dark empty place under a staircase on 56th Street, and fucked him. He started to ask me questions about Spitz's father. I realized he had engineered the whole scene, became terrified, grabbed my clothes and ran away."

Peter Peter's very silent. His mouth turns down at the edges, increasing the wrinkles at the edge of his mouth; he looks like he's upset. I begin to feel guilty, then angry at him.

"Well, what's the matter with you. What do you care if I fuck someone else?"

"Three to zero. You're winning."

"O. Last night we both fucked. Loulou and Julie."

"That was a drag."

I can't disagree with him. My hangover's killing me; and I haven't had enough sleep. I sleep enough only when I sleep until noon, no matter what hour I fall asleep. Since I changed my name, my life's been regulated according to that principle.

I don't want to hurt Peter Peter, but I can't pretend that in the future I won't fuck whoever I feel like fucking. Does he think he can control me? I'm just being guilty, Jewish heritage, I should never pay attention to my emotions. I could be going crazy.

Peter Peter walks along 57th Street where the rich people live, eat, and shop, silent, very silent. Various poorer and tougher saleswomen and waitresses are rushing past him, going to work.

"I have to be alone." Peter Peter says. "I need three or four days to think matters over, matters about myself: I need to have my own adventures. I have to do a lot of composing."

"You're angry at me. You're really planning to leave me, dissolve our partnership. Pretend that you're not my brother."

"Don't be silly. You can't run away from your own family, and I love you. I'm a bit angry; not angry, just jealous; but that emotion hardly matters. I'm not that childlike. I need to be by myself, do composing, do whatever I want to do. I'll return to the hotel room in exactly 96 hours. I'm worried about this detective business. I don't want you getting yourself into some mess, or getting hurt while I'm gone. I guess you don't want to wait until I return to begin investigating the massage parlor. Promise, dear, that you'll be careful."

We puke simultaneously. I feel happy again, want Peter Peter to stay.

"I'm really leaving," Peter Peter says. "Kiss me good-bye."

I don't want to do anything, but I can't leave him until he leaves. I caress him with my eyes, my hands, anything I can, hoping to keep him another minute, another second. Now it will be Rip-off Red, alone.

"Don't try to follow me."

He turns, walks east, down 57th Street, turns around the brown corner. I don't see him again. I don't feel anything.

Like a robot I decide not to follow Peter Peter, I begin to walk west on 57th Street again, toward my hotel room. I'm never going to see Peter Peter again. Do I want to cry, of all things? A tear appears in my eye, falls down my cheek. I brush it away. A flood of tears roll down my cheeks and neck, I might as well get this over with: I bawl and scream my way past Bonwit Teller, across Fifth Avenue, past Miller's Shoes and Bergdorf's. Old men, almost ghosts, passing by me, gasp at me lecherously. As suddenly as I started crying I stop. No more Peter Peter, partner, no more detectives, no more Rip-off Red.

The stores and the people become progressively sleazier and more interesting. Do I have a right, no matter how poor I am, no matter how kicked in the face, shat upon by idiots, abandoned and torn to shreds by the cruel winds of fate, do I have any right whatsoever to abandon Sally Spitz, to let the massage parlor rook other innocent husbands and family men? I'm not another robot, caught in the meshes of this insane society. I'll investigate the massage parlor, alone, tonight; I'll tell them I want a massage. First, I'll baby myself, I'll go back to sleep.

Like some rich dame I quickly hail a cab, fall back into the backseat in my thick silver furs. I wave my hand: order the cab to move. I try to see the New York I knew when I was a child. I can't. I reach my hotel room: I barely notice the room's a mess, too messy even for me and Peter Peter, there's no Peter Peter, as if there's been a burglary: I reach bed, my golden baby pillow, and fall asleep.

Nightmares I'm endlessly abandoned and betrayed by lover after lover, I live on the streets of New York without money a gang of boys drive a stake through my eyes in a fight I'm blind I live in a shed with a jazz player who helps me to live again, to begin to paint and become world famous, wake me up, screaming. I'm in a strange hotel room, drawers pulled out of paper dressers, velvets, silks, Peter Peter's clothes scattered over the room, my precious books strewn across the floor, torn. I suddenly remember: when I entered this room after Peter Peter abandoned me, I noticed something wrong. In the interest of my own mental and physical safety, I better finish this investigation. Fast. Who ransacked my room? And hard work will help me forget Peter Peter. I'm a detective: I have to think and act like a detective at every moment. 6:00. Get to the massage parlor soon so I don't run into Spitz's father. Don't do anything to let the massage parlor bosses know I have any connection to Spitz's father. Spit in their faces.

ELEGANCE: As I walk toward my closet, I see, in the right-hand corner of the hotel room, a long open knife. I pick it up: I can't see any fingerprints. Phooey. The yellow sky outside the windows gives way to gray, at the top, to deep dark gray. I'll have to disguise myself as a society woman: A pair of khaki wool pants cut an inch below my waistline, not tight, straight fall to the floor. A white thick satin shirt, slightly tailored below my breasts, and a blue wool jacket which looks like a man's jacket. On my left wrist, a wristwatch and hidden in the lining of the right side of the jacket, a tiny tape recorder and a thin switchblade. That's all that's necessary. I'll have to carry a shoulder bag with some money and makeup in it, for looks, throw heavy clunky heels on my feet. Lousy to do detective work in. At least I don't have to appear too feminine: the massage parlor bosses are probably too stupid to expect that.

Next I carefully examine my face in the mirror of the bathroom. I look like a Spanish kid. I rub some oil on the back of my neck, brush some brown powder between the skin below my eyebrows and the top of my eyelids. Just like the models do. Paint the skin above the brown white; below the brown, blue. I rub the extra color off with my fingers.

Tiny black dots between each of my lashes to enhance my gorgeous eyes and a bit of black rolled onto my lashes. No need to touch those eyebrows. Blue cupids and fountains painted blue fly over my face. Diamonds on my cheekbones. I paste purple feathers on my lips. Fifteen minutes' work, and I don't look like I've used any coloring. A good disguise. I might even happen to fuck someone tonight, at the parlor, for a brief moment forget Peter Peter. I can't. Sexual contacts don't work that way.

I daintily hail a cab, again, and watch the Big City, streaming by me like a mad subway, the sky now purple, almost black, with a huge white moon behind the tall buildings, each building whizzes by me with a head stuck out of one of the buildings, a body falling out of each window PLOMP, each tall streetlight whose end is visible and shines out at night. We swerve to the right around a red car, sharply to the left, turn down 47th Street, past suddenly lit areas of concrete which are empty, past broken bottles and a famous bookstore a few of the elite are entering, past white hospitals on Park Avenue, tiny expensive French restaurants and brothels; ahead of us, the lights of the United Nations gleam white against the black river. Someday I'll have to sightsee this dump. As we approach First Avenue, I hear crazed drivers screech their brakes, honk their horns to bits. We almost run into a tall man, race around three cars to avoid a jam, in one minute reach our destination: the Irish Saloon. I let my fears increase my excitement, open the creaking wood door, and walk inside the bar.

I walk slowly, back straight, one hand on my leather satchel as if I'm nervous but not too nervous, to the door hidden in back of the bathrooms. The heavy door surprisingly opens; I walk up the stairs, don't race; I'm stepping on the thick ivory-gold carpet in the room full of mirrors.

"Can I help you please? Uh, we're not exactly looking for help, but, considering your looks, if you come by here around noon tomorrow, I'm sure the manager Mr. D'Argent would like to see you."

"I don't want to work here, I want to meet the women who work here."

"Of course. A half-hour massage costs fifty dollars. An hour massage a hundred dollars; we'd prefer if you'd pay now. You may use one or more women, as you please, for your massage. Please fill out this form, you need not give your real name."

Another robot. She whispers into a black box which whispers back to her. I have to remember I'm primarily a detective.

"Uh, I'm a bit nervous. Do you think you could tell me something about this joint before I, ah, get my massage?" I'm good at pretending I'm nervous.

"I'm sorry: I can't help you in any way." Her short hair falls straight to the middle of her ears. A different woman than the one I met the last time I was here. "Please turn left into the corridor; the last room down the corridor is yours."

The thick carpet muffles my footsteps. I walk slowly down the corridor, looking for clues; I hear nothing, see no one. I see a small wood door like all the other doors; I peer to my right and left, listen, slowly turn the knob of the door. I open the door inch by inch, I don't really expect trouble but I want to be careful; I look around the back of the door. Nothing. The walls of the room and ceiling are covered with paisley Indian drapes, gold light, streaming through the drapes, casts weird shadows on the floor. I run my wine-soaked hands through my short hair, and lie down on a small mattress.

I'm too old to care about the romantic aspects of sex. People my age are too lonely and too hermetic: they take what they can get, then leave it. I tend to be a bit schmaltzy about women through lack of experience, but as for males, I want to fuck about three guys a year. I like to approach whoever I want to fuck, I don't like men putting out continual signals for me, messing up friendships; whatever guy I want to fuck wants to fuck me. Attraction's always mutual. Unless the guy's gay, or has a dislike for some general group which he thinks I'm a part of.

"I've been thinking about you constantly; I'm so glad you came here to see me."

I scream, look around, see a tan business suit, a pair of slim hands. Look upward: a chin with a day's growth of dark hair, a thin boyish face, dark curling hair. Manuel. I bet he's the manager of this so-called massage parlor.

He sits next to me; his thighs touch my thighs. Slim hands hold my chin upright. I can't help myself, I want to fuck him again. His large brown eyes look into mine as if he's a child; the corners of his mouth turn upward toward his eyes. I want his lips to touch the lids of my eyes, the deep quivering hole in my belly, the soft thick lips of my cunt. I want him to hold me: to make me, my mouth in an O, the rest of my face squeezed an old nut, come, and come, and come. His face moves slowly toward my face. His lips hover an inch from my lips; his face moves slowly backwards.

His slim hands take off my jacket, fold the jacket neatly over a corner of the mattress, begin to unbutton my satin blouse. I don't want to stop him from undressing me because he might be about to fuck me and help me. I can't start hating myself.

He draws the satin blouse over my body, off me, lays the blouse on top of the folded jacket. The third finger of each hand runs down the sides of my heavy breasts, stop, touches each of my nipples, lightly. Manuel smiles. He draws two lines in my skin from the inner edges of my breasts to my navel; he quickly undoes the hook of my pants, unzips my pants. He sees my hands moving into my pants to help him take my pants off; he slaps my hands, holds them still, on the mattress away from my body. He slowly rolls my body over on its left side, moves to my feet, quickly pulls the pants off my body, lifting my thighs quickly to help him. He lifts his hands flat in front of my face, runs them down my body, the sides of my body, one inch from my skin. He then lays his hand on my cunt, with two fingers, outlines my lips.

He moves to the foot of the bed, bends over, undoes the straps of my huge leather sandals, slips them off my feet. His hands lightly outline the skins around my cunt and the hairs of my cunt; he again smiles extends the third finger of his right hand, puts the tip of the finger between my lips, against my clit. He lays my body on top of his body so that my hand looks like his hand. His finger moves slowly in circles around the flesh inside my lips, circling into my clit which begins to throb. I feel the insides of my knees warm, then my upper legs, then the muscles around my cunt. My legs turn outward, throwing my ass against him, opening the lips around my clit so he can touch me more easily.

Manuel moves his left hand under my wet buttocks. Inserts a finger up my ass. I let go I concentrate on my clit, then on an image of myclit, then on an image of desire. The orgasm begins in my ass, the swirling mass of vibrating walls through the thin skin separating my ass and my cunt, to the shaft of my cunt, quick, ends in my clit, at my clit, spiraling flames that turn on themselves, and die.

"You are so beautiful: I'm glad I've given you pleasure. I would like to be with you, like we are now, all night, but I fear I have to kill you." Before I can understand, he grabs a rope from under the mattress, yanks the rope around my fists, then around my feet so that my back is arched.

"You were given warning to drop this investigation, and you didn't," Manuel continues. "You could easily, with your ridiculous attachment to a dead girl, have gotten yourself into trouble; now I have to help you, and make life easier for you. Monsieur Hawk, Ltd. of which I am the head is not only a massage parlor, but a front for an international and murderous conspiracy. I will personally have to decide whether to turn you into a useless vegetable or kill you. I hope you're satisfied with the trouble you've caused me." His thin face looks sad and drawn.

"I don't want to kill you, but I have to. You'll be well-treated until your demise. However, if your friend ever steps into the Irish Saloon, much less the massage parlor, he will be instantaneously murdered.

"You shouldn't have come here alone."

Manuel smiles, rubs his cock, and quietly leaves the room. I hate myself; I want to kill myself, I want to forget I ever had to go through this misery. Against the soft drapes, I see Peter Peter's face, a knife stuck through his right eye, blood drips down his cheek.

18. May 5, May 6

Fear.

I have to get out of the room, this parlor fast. These creeps could really be about to murder me, dump my body into the garbage eels of the East River, bye-bye Rip-off Red. They probably hate women. I'll show them: I'll blast their massage parlor to hell, I'll throw their so-called macho conspiracy wide open. I'll enter the massage parlor, a huge huge Beretta under my arm, bam, bam, bam; the boss shit falls to the floor writhing agony. My fear and anger enable me to move, roll to my wool jacket; with my teeth, I find the knife hidden in the lining of the jacket, try to push the knife up, through a tiny hole of the lining. Nothing happens. I chew at the blue wool, trying to reach the knife. Those evil creeps are going to return and murder me.

I look around the room for any furniture with sharp edges, bottles I can smash, pieces of metal on which I can cut my ropes. The room has only huge pieces of drapery and a mattress. Those creeps are going to enter this room, stick long sharp knives through my tender skin until the tip of one of the knives touches my heart. I have to escape this joint: my brains are dissolving. I roll over to the door, kick my feet flat aginst the door, hard as I can. I scream and scream scream.

One minute. A hand thrusts open the wood door, slams me against the wall. "Where the fuck are you, whore?" A huge black figure walks into the room, looks around. "I'm going to bust your guts out, whore." The giant listens, walks over to my bruised body. Politician's face looks down at me. "I'm going to bust your guts out." The last event I remember is a slight movement in the corner of my left eye, a tremendous shock against my left ear. I don't remember anything else.

I'm supposed to be telling the truth here. Maybe I don't give a damn for the truth, or can't distinguish between my memories of actual events, fantasies, and dreams. My memory's not so good either. I think slowly; I usually take 24 hours to think through an idea or group of ideas; I don't like to think too much at all. My mother, when she used to lie, which she always did, would tell such ridiculous lies that no one could challenge her. She was beautiful, and mean to me.

I see the door to the room open; a gray figure walks through the hole. Black circles like the waves of a lake ebb from a spot on the left side of my skull; each time the circle breaks against my skull, I feel pain. My mouth's been torn apart. I can take anything. Maybe another person will kick me into oblivion. The gray figure moves toward me: I hear the click of a knife, opening. My hands are free; I can straighten my back, stretch my body across the floor. I look up, my left eye's shut tight, see a face formed by a quarter-inch long brown hair, huge brown eyes. A woman who looks exactly like me. I must be dead.

"I've been ordered to bring you food; I've cut your ropes so you can eat. If you try to get away, I'll have to kill you as painfully as possible."

"Shit yourself up the ass. I haven't done anything." I watch her sit down on the mattress, idly finger a gun. I can now taste the blood in my mouth. A knife's cutting through my soft skin, again and again. My eyes look into my eyes and smile at me, "My name's Laine. I've been working for Manuel for five years."

"How fucking old are you?"

"I was alone in New York, starving in a room in Harlem,

Manuel met me through a friend, gave me money and then a job: I persuade women to work here, not that they need much persuasion, the money's the best in New York for this sort of job, and help design and keep the looks of the place, the food, help the women with their makeup, clothes, get rid of the weirdos. You know. I don't give massages: I'm not able to do that sort of work. But I'm handy with a gun."

"I was born in New York," I venture. "I was a wild kid, but now that I'm old, I lead a calm life. Except, uh, for tonight."

"When I was a kid I lived in Chi, my parents were typical Gentiles, stingy, as repressed and violently horny as robots usually are. When I was 11, I ran around with this motorcycle gang. One of the guys was hot for me, I knew it, but I didn't want to fuck him. I was the only virgin in my class."

I watch the top of her lip press against her nose when she shows disgust.

"One day I was riding on the back of this guy's motorcycle, the whole gang; we were riding by a field. The guy turned his bicycle into the field, asked if for once and for all I'd let him fuck me. 'No.' He told me if I didn't let him fuck me, he and his whole gang would rape me. I started racing through the tall corn. He was furious; he stuck a long three-pronged fork through my right hip."

"Did you let him fuck you?"

"Well, afterwards, after I had stopped bleeding, they gang-raped me. They thought I was going to die."

"Jesus Christ. You must be fucked up. Were you able to fuck again?" Her short hair sticks straight out from her head.

"Chicago bored the shit out of me. This old doodad schmuck told me that he was a famous Hollywood producer, he could make me famous. It's possible to become famous only in New York. If I went with him to New York, he'd set me up for various studio tests, he'd buy me the right clothes and show me what to do. He had white hair, and no cock; he liked to pour wine over me in bed: I was 16 years old. Anything was better than nothing."

"You could have been raped again."

"I came to New York, discovered he knew nobody; he expected to keep me chained to the legs of the bed. One day I found a file, and escaped. I was no longer interested in fame: I didn't know what to do. I cut my hair off, as I am now, and ran for Harlem."

"When I lived in New York," I reply, "before I changed my name to Rip-off, I used to escape from my parents and my school, every afternoon, and systematically walk up and down a different New York street. I wanted to be invisible so I could find out about everything. The guys I knew could do whatever they wanted to in the open; every summer they traveled to South Africa, or they met international artist stars; I had to sneak around and pretend, just to find a fuck. I hated being a female, but I didn't want to be a male either. Once I saw a gin-bum, they can be more malicious than whiskey-bums and winos, wave his bottle in a poetry reading tell the poet what the poet was doing wrong. All great American poets have been gin-drunks: Whitman, Crane, Antin. It's true: the bum was a great poet. He shook all the men's hands, and told the woman who was managing the reading she was a Kotex-ridden bitch. I followed the bum to the corner of a parking lot, where he lay down in some rags, whispering that he was the beginning of a revolution in the United States. The hoboes of the world were going to save the world.

"I sneaked away to elegant drunken bars and then puked in the elevators of rich houses, to co-ops in which poor guys made beautiful dirty films, to poor hotel rooms inhabited by junkies and burlesque stars. Only after I left home and school, and changed my name, could I begin to tell the truth. Since that time, I hate lies."

"You know," Laine says, "I look like you. Your hair looks like mine only yours is curly. Your eyes are as large as mine, and clear; you're my height and weight. You could clunk me over the head, put on my clothes, and run, only you wouldn't escape."

"Why not?"

"Have some more wine. You're beautiful: your eyes and your hair are swirling out through my eyes; you've visited the same silver lands as I have, lands ruled by Silver Gold. You're unable to fuck a guy until you, by repeating his name over and over, convince yourself he's the person you think he is. You don't want to fuck guys who are tall and muscular, look and act strong."

"I want to get out of here, Laine, I'm going to be murdered."

"You don't sleep well at nights. You wake up early in the morning, 7:00, you have to feel you're alone. You're always scared strangers will think you're as crazy as you think you are. I'm scared some person, male or female's going to stick icy green fingers into my brain, make me do everything I'm scared to do. 19th-century 1950s schmaltz puke." She walks over to me; her hands cover my face. "I want you, and I'm going to have you."

I look into my eyes, I'm looking straight up at the palms of my hands:

We're different people. I need to have her hold me, I need to have her hand stroke me until I calm down, I need to have her kiss me, touch me with her lips, until she brings me to orgasm. I need to stroke her, to watch her face pucker, I need to kiss her until she enjoys me, I need to caress her lips until she comes. I'm scared and I I'm not scared:

I raise my head until it's an inch from Laine's head, I place my lips on her lips. She puts her arms around my shoulders, presses my upper body against her breasts and shoulders. I feel terrific. Her tongue, the tip of her tongue, then her whole tongue slides over my tongue, curls to the right under my tongue, as my tongue curves to the right, and around it, until I can no longer tell how our tongues are moving. I thrust my tongue again and again into her liquid mouth.

She reaches down to the cold floor, with an open knife cuts the ropes around my ankles. I fall to the floor against her; again I put my arms around her, place my swelling lips on her mouth. She presses her lips into mine: liquid streams from her mouth into my mouth, then back to her; our tongues again push each other back and forth, until each of our taste buds can feel the skin of the other's tongue pulse.

"Laine, what do you want out of me? What d'you want me to do?"

"We're different from each other." She lays down on top of me so that her mouth touches the mouth of my cunt, she licks the flesh of my inside legs, the line of skin between my leg and the edge of the hair, the thin dots of flesh between each wire. I follow doing to her whatever she does to me. The tip of her tongue outlines the lower edge of my hair her fingers pull the hair away from my cunt lips I feel her wet the hills of my red outer lips. Her tongue dives between the outer lips as three of her fingers enter the canal of my cunt. My feeling of pain changes to a feeling of pleasure. Her tongue touches my clit, too quickly, a long beginning desire for orgasm follows the initial pain of her touch. She circles within and on the thin red lips, over and over the same ground, her fingers press in spirals against the walls of my cunt, pulling at the membrane around and over the clit until the cut begins to grow and throb.

I concentrate on giving her pleasure. My lips touch the lips of her cunt, I lick the flesh of her inside legs, the line of skin between her leg and the edge of the hair, the thin dots of flesh between each slender hair. The tip of my tongue outlines the lower edge of her hair my fingers pull the thick hair away from her cunt lips I feel the bristly skin around her large outer lips. Burning spasms shoot up and down my spiraling body. As I try to touch the opening of her womb with my fingers, I thrust my tongue between the outer lips of her cunt, onto and within her thin red inner membrane. Liquid gathers in the inner folds of her cunt; I can feel her tiny clit begin to throb against the side of my tongue. I can feel the muscles of her cunt move back and forth, the folds of her cunt shrivel, give way to deeper folds. I move my fingers spiraling in the same way I move my quivering tongue. I can feel the strained walls of my open mouth, the muscle of my tongue at the edge where it turns into may throat about to tear into two. My tongue circles within the thin lips, over and over the same ground, my fingers press against the walls of her cunt, pulling at the membrane around and over the clit until the clit begins to grow and throb.

Her leg and thigh muscles stiffen, she more fully relaxes, my tongue touches the edges of her clit, her muscles stiffen even more, relax, the tip of my tongue begins to press down on her clit as her clit moves against my tongue. I put both my hands on the sides of her thighs. I move my tongue to the beginning of the canal, my tongue circles slowly around the canal, then faster and faster as it moves into the canal, as it presses more fiercely against her walls. Her hands tighten around my head, as mine on her head, and press my face into her cunt.

We come together, again and again until it's dangerous for us to come again.

"Laine," I tell her, "we didn't just fuck for nothing; you have got to get me out of here."

"What if I don't want to?"

"I'm here because I've been following this guy here, Mr. Spitz, who's been coming here every night for the last few months. His daughter asked me to investigate him, two days later she was murdered. I found out that Manuel's been rooking Spitz and is probably responsible for Sally's murder that this massage parlor's a front. Do you know for what? You're working for a murderer."

"I don't know that. But I don't like seeing, making way for, women being mistreated by guys. I don't want you to get hung up on me, once we're outside.

"In the corridor outside this room, there's a secret exit: I know how to open the door to the exit. They might inquire at any time where I am; we'd better move faster. Put on your clothes, forget your shoes in case we contact trouble."

Laine stands against the draped wall: the same height body as I have, the same looks I have. I press my cunt slowly against her cunt.

As we open the door, as I begin to step outside the room, I look up, see above me a thin face, gray hair falls around the face, large piercing eyes look into mine. I recognize Spitz's father.

19. May 6: Early Morning

"**E**xcuse me," I mumble to Spitz. "I have to get out of here."

"My dear, you must be wondering why I'm here and if you'll be allowed to escape. I'm enchanted to see you again, even here; perhaps we could have a glass of wine and relax together."

"Why do you come here every night in secret? Do you know why your daughter was killed?" Good against evil.

"You're being ridiculous; come in here and have a drink with me." He ushers me into another room in the corridor; we sit opposite each other in soft brown leather chairs.

"You're too impulsive, my dear, you probably decide you want to sleep with a man after one hour's acquaintance, phone him to ask him if he wants to sleep you: you don't have any idea if he wants to or not." His large gray eyes swirl into my head. "I'm the secret owner of Monsieur Hawk, Ltd. and the head of one of the units of conspiracies to overthrow the United Nations in New York. I want to tell you exactly what has been happening so that you can decide what side you are on. Your little, uh, excursion with Laine has made this decision necessary, though I am not sure I was planning to murder you. Laine, of course, can decide whether she wants to continue working here or leave. Would you like some wine?"

"Of course. Does Manuel work for you, along with Laine?"

"O the impulsiveness of you young people. I'll tell you the real story from its beginning:

"When my daughter Sally returned to New York, she informed me and my wife that she had met you on the plane, and loved you. Later that night, from a tape recorder I had running in my child's bedroom, I learned that my child had hired you to investigate my activities and that she had told you I was a jeweler and worked for the U.N. Even later that night, I learned by phone call from Manuel that Sally on her own had followed me to the massage parlor and learned of the parlor's existence. One of our workers had seen Sally enter the parlor. I quickly made up my mind. Once Sally was dead, you would drop your investigation."

"You murdered your own child?"

"I'm sure you have murdered at least one person who was dear to you. Think clearly. As artists we must suffer; we walk blind in a black world. I decided that politics, the survival of humanity, was more important . . ."

"Murder is evil. You stopped, stopped forever, Sally's life."

"Have you ever murdered anyone?" Spitz asks me.

I can't answer. I have no more eyes; a knife is plucking out the center of my right eye.

"I'll continue: Perhaps it's purely by chance that I had to fight you. For the next day, when you by chance walked into the crowd around Sally's body, I was in that crowd, and overheard you ask the policemen about me overheard you swear you would avenge Sally's murder. Sally's murder was useless. I stupidly told Manuel, who was with me, to follow you, to scare you away from New York. You have more courage, my dear, than I first thought possible.

"When I formally met you at my dear wife's party, I realized you were both beautiful and dangerous. Even then, I would rather have had you as my ally than my enemy. I still thought that I could evade you: you would never trail me to the massage parlor. Unfortunately I didn't know about your partner's existence; you and your partner together were able to follow me. And if you did follow me here, so what? Many men, obviously," Spitz smiles, "go to massage parlors. Daily, maniacally. No connection existed between my visits to a massage parlor and Sally's murder."

He pours both himself and me another glass of wine.

"I told Manuel to spy on you, meet you and question you. You certainly are a lustful person. Then another mistake occurred. You slept with my wife, and learned from her that I, uh, do not go to massage parlors. You stupidly continued your investigations. By this time, I was carefully following your daily life.

"I am a civilized and brilliant man. I do what I think best in what manner I think best. I never hesitate to stop a course of action once I decide to, or to destroy former hard work. I feel neither guilt nor remorse, only sometimes pride, a little part of pride. Men call me 'tyrant' but I'm not. I live by my own rules as all of us must do. You also.

"You know the end of this part of the story. I told Manuel to scare you badly. Manuel searched your room, and as you were walking toward the hotel, he threw a knife at you. You didn't pay any attention to our threats. You know that when you returned to the massage parlor tonight, I had to stop you, take you forever out of New York. However, Laine decided to help you, and now, my dear, you and I must make some more decisions."

I call up X; ask him to sleep with me. Who are you? O you met me at the poet A's two years ago. When do you want to fuck me, and where? I'll take a vacation; I'll meet you. I'm traveling north slowly; you're welcome to travel with me if you want. I want to be able to return to Y.

"And that, my dear, is that."

"What is the true story?" I ask.

"You're really quite intelligent. As I believe you know, I am a diamond jeweler and a special advisor to an economic counsel, UNUN, the Universal Nuggets of the United Nations. About a year ago UNUN decided to organize a meeting of important artists from all over the world: artists, architects, writers, electronic musicians who could discuss their visions of an ideal universe, visions that could help us more clearly envision our future goals. Thus: our future economic goals. The meeting, by the way, was a failure: the artists continually argued with each other, refused to speak, refused even to appear, and used as much of our fundings for special visitors as they could manage to use. One of the architects, an old old woman named Gaga, in discussions between the two of us, showed me the truth about the international organization I was serving. A deadly organization, CREEP, since the beginning of the U.N., has been infiltrating the U.N., rendering the U.N. unable to stop wars and deadly underground conflicts between nations and peoples, transforming the U.N. into a subsidiary of its own lethal organization. The center of CREEP is in this country and the main attack of CREEP is against the U.N. in New York.

"Let me tell you some things about the structure of CREEP:

"There are two main organizations that compose CREEP: an inner organization and an outer organization."

I start talking about my strange childhood.

"A hierarchy, unlike the conspiracies of which I'm a part. The outer hierarchy, the organization which appears in the media, is made up of gangsters who think they can shoot their way into fame and fortune. Who think a woman is a cunt. The inner organization contains the top men, the almost unknown and unknown men who rule the world and are never connected with crime. These men, unlike the men of the outer organization, act always in terms of their own self-interest.

"A gangster, you see, is a man or a woman who is a robot: if he once acts in his own interest, the inner organization maims or kills him. If he makes a mistake he is likewise maimed or killed. We in the conspiracies, on the other hand, don't believe in hierarchies.

"The structure of the inner organization is as follows:

"Under the head of CREEP are four departments: Affairs in the U.S., Home Operations, The Security Council, and Communications. Under Affairs in the U.S. we find a Domestic Counsel. There is one chief man in Affairs in the U.S. and in the Security Council; the other departments have two chiefs.

"Home Operations is the most important of these departments. It governs four other subsidiary departments: Outside Organizations (one chief), Political (one chief), Counsel to the Head (two chiefs), and. Scheduling (one chief). Outside Organizations controls The Consultant (one chief). The names of the chiefs would mean nothing to you.

"CREEP is subterraneously connected with four legitimate organizations: The Organization of Money and The Organization of Electronic Bugging, Clandestine Photography, and Political Espionage. The key word connecting these three organizations is "jewel." One of the heads of the organizations has to pretend that his wife is mad.

"To return to my former story," Spitz continues, "Gaga, the architect, told me about the conspiracy, or rather the conspiracies, not against CREEP, but for the sake of conspiracy. There exists throughout the world and especially in the U.N. millions of small groups who are trying to maintain the precarious existence of life on this planet. One or more organizers, not heads, and any number of secret members equal in rights to the organizer, make up each of these groups. No group nor conspiracy has a name. At any moment we may or may not, by chance, be in contact with any other group. When Gaga returned to Italy, I decided to form such a group, and did so, using my massage parlor as a front for my real life. Manuel is a member of my group. Or of the group I organized.

"I'm telling you this so that you can come to a rational decision. You are, of course, being asked to join my unit of conspiracy. Or you can try to tell the New York police about Sally's murder."

"Considering your beautiful politics, how could you kill Sally? Why did you kill Sally? I can in no way condone murder."

"I do not either, my dear, usually condone murders. Murderers. It is possible to be forced by extraordinary pressures, sexual pressures, the pressures of fear, to murder another person."

Since I was born, my parents have refused me any affection or assistance. I am too proud to ask. When I was dying, two years ago, they refused to lend me money so that I could see a decent doctor. New York where most clinics stink. If I murdered my parents, I would inherit one or more million dollars.

"I have a dream," Spitz declaims, "a dream of a world in which there are no hospitals, schools, dentist offices, no marriages in which the asshole is as welcome as a cunt or cock, in which men and women get more, are Rockefellers, steal jewels gold bars open banks heist trains haul narcotics masturbate. Of pleasure. I have a dream of morality that is no morality of people who are murderers the streets and buildings of New York turn yellow, the sun and piss, the sky reappears to our sightless eyes. The buildings of New York crumble; the bums and junkies sit on the edges of the sidewalk, stare at the blue sky. Children begin to have sex with each other at the age of two. People do their own minimal work. Drugs and food lie out on the streets, drying slowly into dust and metal. At night, the moon comes slowly walking, a woman, into the new city."

"O.K.," I reply. I pour myself another glass of wine. "So you murdered Sally. I don't care about Sally anymore: she's dead. I don't care about her murder. If I join the conspiracy, I'll have to stop being a detective, I'll exist no more. I'll be a series of wavering energy-forms surrounded forever by other wavering energy-forms. I'll have no identity."

Spitz's hand reaches across the table and holds my hand. "Do you want to join me," he asks me, "and help me?"

"I don't know."

Red jewels flame up in my bleeding hands.

I feel delighted. My mother takes me, both on separate bicycles, to a large area of dirt, a tent that's an open stationery store; magazines line the wood racks. Walk night through the wavering fields through the wavering fields clear grass flat land, south, one or two trees. We want to reach a rundown wood house, half-crumbling house in which people live. I'm at a university: I sit in a chair on an outside terrace, watch rich people in silks and velvets come out for some dance. I'm jealous as hell. Not for me. I walk south to the ocean, I take off my clothes, should I keep my white shirt on? Dive into black waters, too muddy, I walk into a swimming pool. A man who's wearing one pearl earring passes by me. I've been telling my girlfriends I'll tell the guy off: he stole my earring. I give it to him. I jump into an outdoor pool with another woman, the pool's too shallow no the end's deep enough. Yay.

I walk west through two sets of double doors into an enclosed pool. A man approaches me, he looks too much like a jock, he has to teach me how to paint while I float in the pool. I should jump in the water, ankles crossed, smoothly; that way I'll balance above the water. I succeed the first time. I float a piece of cutout paper on the water dip a brush in green paint. Then sprinkle yellow dots over the green. His painting is defined areas green yellow green. Much better. I notice he's got a smaller more easily usable brush. I'll never be a painter.

We get out of the pool he sits in a chair I sit on his lap my back against his stomach I'm naked, he wriggles out of a black bathing suit. Slowly his cock circles inside the beginning of my asshole, the edge of my asshole. I come slow expand explosions stronger and stronger until my nerves a tidal wave burn and burn and burn. I turn around; my his black fur; we quickly fuck.

"Do you want to live with me?"

I feel he's putting me off. "I have to meet X at the rich dance: she's waiting for me."

I turn around, walk away, by myself, through the tall grass.

In a basement, the trick is to jump from rafter to rafter. If I fall from a rafter, I'm dead. A huge ocean below. I grab a vine, swing from rafter to rafter. A huge room with wood beams, a triangular roof. I want to kill the evil woman. I just want to get close to her. A series of abstractions. After I stand next to several women, I manage to reach the evil one. We become friends.

I free my hand from Spitz's hand. I say to him, "I'm not going to join the conspiracy now; I'm going to forget about my acquaintance with you and your family." I want to keep having adventures, I want to be a hermit: work like mad for six months, for one month break loose: fuck like mad, find out everything. I'm not especially interested in being happy. I live on almost zilch money.

I'm no longer a detective. I'll decide to become someone else.

THE BURNING BOMBING

OF AMERICA:

The Destruction of the U.S.

THE BURNING BOMBING

OF AMERICA

The Burning Bombing
of America

armies defect   first in the woods and polluted lakes   the
cities   small towns are covered with the blood of God
in the burrows and hidden alleyways of unknown anarchists criminals buggering and fucking for ages   a monster
arises half green half the color of the new sky   the Mother of
God the new Jesus freak destroys all children all sacred families.
the beginning. children lie in the streets   there is no lying there
is a new day   night-day trees in which are houses   city lights
guns the size of five-story houses with no holes no fireplugs   bombs
exploded ten years before they are made   propaganda so incredibly
beautiful   people are not only individual people   the mosques
are rising full in the air green and orange thin stripes at the edge
of the sky   the churches are huge auditoriums in which thousands of people hear nobody sing Hindu hymns   there are insects   there are animals   a red patch on the outside of the
upper arms tiny dry skin bumps coo-coo   the people are shout-
ing they are protesting give to anyone what she asks for asking
implies need   you lying in bed beside me a person's walking
across us with a flaming machete   the city's erupting   the world's
blowing itself up in three seconds it is going to and you are the
only living being who can stop the explosion you will have to
kill your children a huge fire over our heads yellow-orange flames
there's an angel with endless spreading wings.

*   *   *

when the world turns communist   totally in spirit the opening
of paradise   beginning   trees and water come back   birds   huge
red feathers blue jays mynah birds maggots of purple silk. with
a gold fillet around her cunt the dervish turns round round   cock-
cunt opening into our finger   hair twists into the vines of man-
eating flowers   we open at night with our recorders and turtle
shells we slowly walk on the sky into the white light   down again
into each other's rooms   the peacock opens her tail   scraggly
hair   eyes pop out until there's enough food   a red cat leaps
onto another   licks its head under its neck   its stomach. the cat
makes noise through its nose on a blue silk cover among gold
cupids and flowers on the wall a red-and-yellow poster celebrates
the burning of the banks   yellow sun   the day is coming nearer
the doorbell rings   a rapist runs through the hall knife glitters
cut off cock   we can hear the police sirens through the record
player   he's coming closer no windows to leap out of a fire escape which won't support you one limb cut off bleeding a broken bottle shoved up the cunt causes bleeding in the vagina and
uterus   your neck cut an inch away from the jugular vein   he
comes closer. now. now this very instant the true gold   the light
from the opening of the window   the door   into Arabia the slip-
ping of the veil   he knows thousands of sex acts endless displays
of pleasure while she flies to the moon by herself around her neck
an ancient Chinese scarf.

the paradise of no work   we are part of a decaying world or we
are a new society   and don't know how to act. past time mixes
with future time   the long curtain blows away   Nietzsche walks
arm in arm with the Buddha   they are fucking slowly pushing
long cocks into each other's asshole   grass springs up we walk
past the lanes of flowers in new drag a wild garden in which elephants small deer three black stripes around their asses giraffes

run their whole bodies in the air and swaying. birds come through the air imitating the monkey noise   long strips of the sun are hidden under piles of shit   fermenting leaves cat-children prowl on the second layer of the world   they chase after a rolling dark blue pipe cleaner   meet a midget deformed from a bomb   HISS gold stand up   the stars disappear   underneath the women wait they've waited 3,000,000,000 years   to blow up the cities   slowly cut off each of Nixon's balls   each piece of cement flies off into the blackness   forever gone   each department store splintered into a thousand golden pieces each cancer cosmetic transformed by the stone into pure cunt juice   nectar we have cultivated the flower opens each velvet petal one at a time black and purple and yellow each part of each petal atom by atom smell starts appearing   the fear of getting what we want   sight   touch   hard touch that opens the night   through the gap we see the final city cat-women howl on the bridges houses thin as a lace a bird more fiery than a peacock lights on the top steeple   food that would feed a trillion times a trillion people for that many and more years trees which look like salukis white-and-black spirals   smells of cat-sperm   broken TV sets   chairs made from the spines of czars.

The Betrayal of Friends 1

the first female pornographer's   before the awakening of paradise   we are crying out   we shall get exactly what we want   we shall plant bombs in the assholes of our masters our skins are half arsenic half nitrochloric acid half the velvet of old Chinese sages with writing foretelling our rule. our cats are daggers   they will cut out your eyes   they will slowly unravel your brains   twine them into tiny yarn balls we have invented guillotines   more subtle tortures with maces and ancient racks water falls drop by drop   our junkies roam the streets starved by us made by repressions into rapists our favorite murderers who worship Nixon. money   we carefully search out each human who is not yet a robot   convert him by giving him a job $10,000 a year   he recites dead numbers   this activist first heard answers analytical stomach think we have to have some of our own things in mind. in a small room one man is beating up another man takes the end of the tongs   lifts up   bong   the forehead skin opens   muscles around the legs loosen   he wants more needs body slackens   drool   hands open drip   skin becomes floor muscles tighten   breathing has disappeared   bong   half the teeth gone   blood flows around our mouths and asses we eat down moving meat   worms rise up in our intestines there is no food   there is no way in the future of getting food   we are not women   we are waiting for the beginning   Castro is wrong: if we are living in shit we are in every way made up of shit   junkies the lack of shelter   doctors who won't cure   food roaches refuse friends disappear appear betray me   my gold and leather chains today a boy is shot in the head by cops for running away from a car his mind and body ruined for life.

Communist Aesthetics

the communists are angels against the rich men   they under-
mine their buildings they're destroying art their jaundiced
fucking. they will substitute free food a new bed in which are
dreams   O communists O Silver Women-Men   Cunt I want to
place my head upon Margie is no longer my friend   Harris is
not talking to me   Big Mama Thorton's singing beautiful dyke
in a dream I'm a dyke sleeping with everyone in the world. this
writing is about sex   the thin cock of Paul   Lizzy's long nipples
that I rub slowly with the tips of my fingers making her purr
strange sounds in the house   the animals race back and forth   a
lion caught under a net leaps about paws at the ground he sees
two men coming toward him with two guns lies down on the
ground quiet stares at the men moves back without moving
tensed wide open eyes men cock the triggers of the guns. warm
smells hit the nose carrots and pistachios whole-wheat flour oil
of sesames   the night is all around the red room

The Betrayal of Friends II

how interesting to continue. I'm again not doing anything an animal doesn't do anything not eating not sleeping. I sweat I smell the inside of my arms. diarrhea. bells like trumpets high register on the piano eat something I don't want to how high can you get until writing becomes impossible writing as communication. don't deal with friends don't be in a large room with friends blankets on the walls two rugs on the floor felt pillows so many books in the room no one can sit down a yellow chair swings from the rafters there's a lot of dope untouched cans of beer. a room long and narrow five low tables are on the floor green walls and a green rug a black cat with green eyes slowly walks to the back of the room. in this room Nixon plans the end of the world 400 men in Albany control me. fur fur lights. no bells. I don't want to do anything this has to be perfect a recorder is for playing or betrayal. the two children in the beautiful forest creep into the low house their hands are chained the soles of their feet are beaten with thin horsewhips they are thrown into a closed pigpen fed with pig shit rotten grain. they grow fatter and fatter they pretend to fall in love with the witch she is their mother gradually she believes they love her she lets them play in the house as she bends over a small stove one child puts arms around her waist the other child sticks the head of the witch in the oven they shove her into the oven forever. communist children playing with goats five dogs and five cats in the new forest trees shelter them from the rain plants feed from them as suns.

Communist Story I

I want to talk to you again. you have no desire to talk to me since you do not call me and you were the one to say we shouldn't go to bed together. I don't want to go cruising again at the Firehouse but there's no one around. I pick up a stranger we talk for a half-hour we dance together I go cruising a bit talk to acquaintances we dance more for some reason start kissing trade phone numbers or agree to meet somewhere I want to get the hell out I don't want some stranger fucking into my ordered solitude I don't know why I'm acting insanely. I know who I want to talk to I'm in a mess I don't want to have anything to do with anyone. you're going to be out of New York soon I can sit here and think about anything I want to I can do my best to figure out how to earn money painlessly worklessly I have to get someone new. I've got to start talking again a new moon in my hair and fingers my body made of indestructible magnets. when I say fuck fuck means anything. the Lakers make 55 baskets you sit back and try to make them feel good. anything could happen there's no way to reach you you don't let anyone actually touch you you make sure that you only fuck strangers. the lion the table the apple the wall stone. you opening and closing.

Communist Story II

(for Lenny)

the tailor in the city of New York weaves one thousand pieces of cloth   in and out   through above each other's eyes   green silks and brocades to make his fortune. velvets the touch of your thighs. he has no ears   no eyes   he can hardly walk through the crowded streets where boys steal his money   older men stick fingers into him   he visits the sheep the artists   he gets home smokes on a bed   with one sheet. he hears the goats talking the birds tell him his stories   the stars assure him he will win. when he goes to sleep people are jangling recorders in his ears   brass cymbals   the temple of Solomon collapses at 5:00 in the morning he leans down and captures the sun. stay with me forever. he doesn't want to talk to anyone   he never again will want to lie on his bed with a stranger   touch spires   thin animal ears. cloths of purples and reds gardens in which are talking birds   deer who are half-people   gentler than the other people   royal   cats perched high on the stars   arching their backs. talk to me again they say till me that you won't stop talking to me and leave me blind. I want to kill everyone   I want to take a woman   I want to slice open her throat   stick a jar up her cunt until it fills up with blood. come out sun watch me. he repeats again and again and again   the words are sad the cats lay still and listen. your cunt is beautiful your eyes are inside mine. the animals all fuck

each other don't give a damn who fucks who   any animals fucks
in the head the tail the cunt   they race around fuck again sixty
times a day. the birds chatter among themselves   they know men
will soon disappear   the preservation of the earth   they eat the
insects off of the fur of the animals   fly off to the dying moon.

COMMUNIST NARRATION

among the grass were thousands of apple petals   a slight odor   wet grass and wet dirt the dirt is dark brown or light brown   the sun pulses back and forth into a cone there are two people in the world they remain invisible stick my tongue into the earth. wet jeans on the front of my legs. spill lousy sugar wine into the grass. the thousands of poor people beneath this rich mansion don't exist. light. light. LIGHT.

I'd tell you that I think you're wonderful. I'd like to be with you many hours   I'm scared you'll reject me. think you like me. I haven't talked so openly to anyone in New York   Margie? (blank) Harriet? no. among huge roses red purple   a woman sits   her legs are tied with thongs   her thumbs up GOOD   out of her gorgeous hairy cunt comes a papyrus   a man walks along takes a huge black horsewhip   out of his bag   SWISH   the cats go flying   SWISH   the world is going to be blown up   we are going to make love   when you fall in love everything goes blooey your work doesn't matter anymore (for a while)   SWISH   Lizzy lies on top of the wood commode   she runs a fever glassy eyes SWISH   I'm going to talk about politics or about anarchy   the beautiful blowing up of the United States how the revolution started   in the dismal days   the first explosion of the mansion the gradual increase of arsons   murders   planned forays into the forests   squirrels in winter   strawberries   green apples   cherries we stop to buy a pint of Jack Daniel's   there's always time for that   we wander among green trees looking for some room or some number a man with a small beard   we don't want any of these to happen.

black kid sneaks in the door in back of me   arms grab my arms just as I'm opening the elevator   DON'T TOUCH ME   WHY ARE YOU TOUCHING ME   come into the elevator with me I won't hurt you   race up stairs   second floor going to race up back stairs elude rapist   back stairs are less open   stand by three doors   doorbells protection look around   black kid comes out of elevator   I'm about to press three doorbells   he disappears super's house   there's a guy in the building somewhere   he attacked me once   a black kid   go away   I don't want anything to do with anybody   out comes my police whistle   look around go to front stairs   look up them to next floor   race up stairs three times   Jerry's apartment a guy attacked me in the front hall he's somewhere in the building   will you come down here don't have any clothes on   go to hell   after a while you learn the rules of the jungle   you don't wear heels that click   you're always ready to scream   Jerry comes up to get some Giorno poems   what destruction are you discussing   L(enny) isn't talking to me   I'm not acting in a way conducive to his desire to fuck B(ernadette) his desire to rule the world   O beautiful blowing up of the U.S.! happen! happen!

new day. the war has begun. man all battle stations number two the enemy is escaping   come forward   announce your names; wear rings   pins   blue jeans   announcing your name. don't stop talking to me. the first level has started exploding   mass murder is a way of touching   we are floating on yellow clouds we are always in touch with each other   these are the words of strangers   friends   don't kid yourself   don't kid yourself   we might (probably) not get out of this alive   we have to know exactly what we are doing   we have to be aware at all times.

I go to Grand Street to give B. a book   *Destroy She Said*   you're here to use me all you want is to sleep with me you must not like me   I know you're upset about E.   my skin turns white   the bathroom   I feel horrible   I feel lifeless   I sit against a cold bathtub on the tile floor   safe   no desire to move   many hours pass I stand up almost faint   can't remain in this enemy territory   I have to get from the bathroom to the door without fainting down the stairs   faint   wake up   pain from my right ankle ask E. who has followed me down noticing my faintness to get a cab to get to Beth Israel   in spite of the tremendous pain I remain coherent and conscious. an hour later   shock. two hours later L. calls B. they're not coming over tomorrow   B. and E. are going away this summer. I live on a planet   the temperature ranges from –10 to 50°F. red purple lichens   ice moons govern my thoughts desire   I'm equal to strange animals   the long-clawed cats the insane children   I'm the only human   I sleep well   I dig up my clothing   thongs around my ankles   my nails two inches long   I lie on the grass a stake through my heart I am every woman   this is my insane blood   I don't have anything else to give you   listen   listen   sound waves animal waves light waves. these are all fantasies. I'm on my way through the city until I finally pass out   die   I can tell you how disgusting everything is   actually I talk only to H. and J.   I don't know B. and E. at all except to know they don't want to know me   I know many people that way   I know thousands of people who don't want to know me and want my nookie   I've heard about real criminals (saints are in the jails) ، black woman screams in hall words inaudible   make the building fall   this is what is happening   at this point   I don't tell lies.

at night H. takes a needle   sticks needle into her thumb hard as she can   traces out with her red liquid the figure of her friend   long feather pipe   endless pieces of cloth   mixed with water   the hospital is dead quiet   the bathrooms are filled with green puke   through the heart of a woman she drives a pointed stake   don't you see   don't you see   takes it out   again   again   I am serving her   the cocks are larger than the moneyed spires   the black woman still screeching   the sleeping pills of the city don't work. on TV young girl-older man   they're going to get married   older man's wife   comedy   why don't you laugh   at night H. wanders from bed to bed like a zombie   the man too sick to walk three feet to the nurses' station a cop finally threw him out for loitering a guy dying of TB   Mr. Phooey you haven't taken your good medicine and now you're going to die   a woman puking her guts out from an ulcer   nembutal and synthetic opium is for all patients despite the lack of medicine   a black woman in a pink black nighty when they get out of the hospital she'll call H. every day   I pay H.'s rent wrongly?   let my husband see your picture he's seen sex pictures before   too scared to return have to make a lot of money to pay rich doctor   we take their pain-killers   make dirty movies   display our gorgeous vaginas to any $5-head on filthy bed-cover stage   we are managing to stay conscious. on welfare Medicaid check H. has tooth pulled doctor looks for root to see if he still remembers how to find a root   H. is now dead. H. is sitting in a 9' × 9' white tile box I'm not strong enough to help her. H. is chained hand and foot   she's screaming   I'm trying to earn some money she's in a brothel changing the beds of whores $25 a throw   she has to let the men have her free   she's flying to the moon. the cats are sleeping this is the truth   1971–1972   you're a bunch of milk-white turds.

(end of diary)

this is to be (an end) rest. moon. is waiting until the waters are about to overflow. the evil city is waiting. H. hasn't fucked in a year. out of the rubble   huge snakes   the noncolor of jellyfish raise their heads above me   open white jaws. the secret passage-ways in the rubble   women give their breasts to rubber dolls if you kiss someone   on the subways   old men   pants unzipped cocks waggle at you   hello hello   there's no night a yellow gray sky   you go home at dawn   the evil magicians are out to kill you with huge lobotomy needles   the evil magicians who at will fly away. O dense city   Monster spawning trillions of worse Monsters   Evil Knife   you destroy all rest   you make dreams purple   GET RID OF MIND   you make farmers hide in the trenches   their wives will prostitute get rid of the Germans their wives-concubines make *pot-au-feu* onion soup with cups of cheese pâtés   sugar *gateaux*   for our wedding   our dance of delight which is starting   recorders   flutes   drums   cymbals   lyre   sax the wines we have spent a hundred years fermenting   the trodden hay. a parade begins the wedding   two goats enter first   fucking geeks   all the poets who think they're immediately changing the world spontaneously creating food   all the whimpering sobbing idiots $ big fat   doctors lawyers teachers   the shits who keep the world ongoing   the wedding cake is of come and the bride   the bride   her mother is crying   there's already been trouble   it doesn't matter who you marry no marriage can possibly last longer than three years   I want another wedding veil   I especially want to look beautiful   what is communism about? the desire of the heart for

155

more than one love. this is the end. the city cursed for a thousand years is destroyed by a man who can't walk   a stupid man   deer-cat-man   doesn't talk so well   last son man

he walks into the town he's too stupid to say thank you   he takes out his pipe and plays. many hours pass by. here blood flows as easily as sex.

a place of rest. end. 5/72

II Diary

Only the heart satisfies   the destruction of the world   we cut off our right legs   joined by our fingertips   world/world/world   we are walking past the toilets piled on ash heaps   fires now reduced to small blazes   the children are dead   we are talking to each other we are in bed fucking each other this is only good if I make it true   if it is a diary   if I stop lying stop giving a shit about the quality. your women likewise are becoming monstrosities   legs longer than the exaggerated ones of a model   arms thrown back breasts thrust out   your women are the results of your insanity as much as this desire of mine. no more trivia   we don't have time for trivia. the beautiful crap   pictures   the bullwhips we handle   from and twirling them up   our cunts   they have to begin to lash. this is a doctrine call it what shit you want. I'm not thinking anymore I've given up spelling   syntax   image   beginning   the colonnades   holy sun   holy moon   that's what I was showing you energy is us to be used so it becomes more energy   nurse myself holy mother and child   MY CUNT   second   pain   make it as good as possible. 1. the cunt is the beginning. 2. guts and energy. 3. the black hair   the city   the hatred   sex   continuous disgusting apocalypse. I was going to stop writing to gather the energy   unable to function   unable to have sex   keep the concentration specific   yoga good exercise   this working a way of living. keep aware at all times. no discipline is absolutely necessary   it is everything. this is written at midnight imaginary conversation with H. (from real conversation with H.)

*   *   *

beginning of journey-diary through the puke lower world. the
desire of the city. evil desire for the end of the day   the magicians spread their poisons   there is no light left   no smooth velvet flesh   the wise man decides not to move   split mountain/
water   you and I   two hands move slowly across the plain. in
the desert we come to an old water station   ghost station town
glowing red snakes pulling up some water   feed drops to the dog
convulsions   his skin blows up into shreds   we live inside the
skeletons of horses   clothes of vulture feathers   wait for the
bomb. you're coming out of the anesthesia   a child   your wet
cunt   needles stuck in your arm   where are we? I don't want to
write anymore   I'll just talk   forget it   inspiration gone   energy
high   general feeling in the consciousness: can't get myself together   what are you doing   I'm flying into outer space   I'm
going insane. 25 mg. Valium   one seconal.   50mg. Benzedrine
unknown chemicals in the food   personality changes result. hospitals are for getting well. don't believe it   don't believe anything
you hear. be as paranoid   schizophrenic   as possible. all sen-
tences suspect. Stupid Man says the universities are in league with
the evil magicians   the so-called Death Wards   Columbia deals
arsenic-napalm   DD3 welfare means lobotomy   nurses are robot-
ants. Allow people to do whatever they want   allow the streets
to be covered with silk   people will dance wildly in the streets
in the first world balloons will sail through the heads of angels
dreams will be alive   at 3 A.M. this morning. we shall lick each
other's sweet cunts without fear   our cunts are the fur of animals cat-animals   I tell you   I want this to happen   this would
be the destruction of the city.

(for H. in the hospital)

is this in no place gentle? end of the journey. rubble piles of the shit of the poor   green vomit   clouds and darkness are around us   the cat-weather (wo)men rise up   are killed   arise from the dead   there is no stopping now   with huge whips we walk on the dogs   the parks have died   our legs gone   through our own and everyone's blood   through masses of insects   the ship leaves the harbor like a knife   sapphire water   through the empty buildings of the kings   where now huge cats eat the leaves. nipples rub against the stone   she raises her head   endless curls thrown back   her fingers caress planets (we no longer know what's happening) 1. matter exploded   the separate spheres rush away from each other through space 2. matter is continuously spontaneously creating itself in the center of the universe 3. through holes in the universe enters the matter of other universes. the mind disappears   she throws out her arms   cat at every pore cats whose tails are curled around the dirt of the three worlds. but gentleness has to be our real life. writing is the use of information without the source of the information. Heaven gives to the deficient   takes away from the abundant   men   the evil magicians of the city   prey   blood-crazed parasites   the poor. can't get hold of people anymore. is velvet soft? do plants yield? cats love human-people. the rug disappears beneath the feet   we both want someone to sleep with   Bob Dylan shits out money

notice where the money is   you'll find out where the killers lie
the men who are annihilating the universe   don't joke   you're
recovering   recovering from the hatred of the doctor   how does
one (we) recover? what is happening? L. sits on top of the book-
case   P. on the blue table   Y. in her home   noise from the
radio and the street   L. is asleep (no information)   the Tao   Te
Ching: excess leads to bad things.

we search out the evil magicians with sharpened knives   a rest
we lie in wait. end of the first discussion of my first   gentlest love.

the cry of desire   now make a movie

too much noise   endless swarms of people   the elevator plunges
and destroys ten old women   H. is in touch with the Big Man
and the Big Lady   end the War   end the War   Spanish people
dancing on the concrete under my city body   happy people
happy people   move the muscles around the clit   each part   B.
and H. and G. and T. and L.   who's going insane? who's scared
to the point of insanity? refuses to ask help   who's so lonely for
actual touch/discussion? won't find anyone to open to   die on
the spot. you fuck-puke nonperson   you think your preach language says anything human/real   you think all human thoughts
and desires not directly concerning the Vietnam War are not real
needs   indications of insane emptiness. I'm going to call you up
this evening   I was paranoid you'd take away my reading   you
don't like my work. I hurt. you're pure strength because you say
one thing   to kill the Evil Magicians   communism is needed
endless sex   the cycle of the weather and plants   the meeting
of the inside and outside of all. food and shelter. people who when

they show they love you   love you. this is this Sunday. this is a
communistic Sunday   as usual I'm alone   went past the Firehouse   cruising   back to safe territory   subway home safer territory (cats)   I don't want to be alone   I know no other way of
being   I disguise   even now to myself my desire ((disguised))
revolutionary sex-love-lust. huge cats prowl inside my toes and
legs   they're at war   extend claws through my cunt   the elevator   planks of wood with a string tied in the middle   rises
up   in one side I hold on to the string   a stranger holds on to
the string on the other   the stars rush away from each other at
rates proportional to their distance from the center of the universe   these are the Evil Magicians: not only the Vietnam War
every fucking minute   every desire that cannot be filled   now
now   now   now   now   now. these are the enemy you stupid
schmuck nonyoga knowing schmuck   I change identity   I'm
climbing up the stairs to A.W.'s apartment   I trip   I fly away
the jewels of the night glow in your hands   your bones come
through your skin   huge prowling feet   your night and sound
your armpits are covered with the human skin of your lovers   you
rise to the center of the universe.

and then   the city arises   rises from your cunt   golden star
there are no buildings but silk and thick cotton tents   animals
deer with hands for legs run down the pavilions   people with
them   at the same rate. there are no families   but centers   warm
breast   living person when I need to have my muscles lifted out
placed on a flat surface   rubbed   I need to have socks put on
my feet by L. so by the morning I fall asleep   no families ruin
the hearts of women and men by forcing them through torture
to desire   outlawed desires   you are healthy again   you are
able to run with two legs   the doctor who killed you has stopped
killing you   what of the politicians   what of the layer of weapons like streams hidden beneath the streets $ has become an
image $ has become an illusion   dream followed by 1% of the
population   bad acid-speed   no drugs are necessary   L. and I
no longer fuck   what will happen in one week? the new city
arises   I place diamonds in the hair of your cunt   you who
I can desire   birds with red and purple feathers grow out of
the branches of trees   on one small tree   one inch below each
branch   hang strings of yellow flowers   berries and tea for
breakfast   huge peaches   savory grass   heartease   purple basil
rue   tansy (poison)   laurel   cinnamon   olive tree   lamb's ears
quince   spearmint   parsley curled mint   forget-me-nots   rose-
mary   summer savory   wild grass   chives bloom into purple

flowers   we are extremely irritable   it becomes easier not to deal
with people   to tell people we're not home   we find it difficult
to stay alive   in the distance   to the left   the old witch ran after
us   a huge stick surrounded by metal spikes in her hand   she
changed into a small white bird   a huge fish in the pond we had
to jump across   a fat townsman tried to make his horses kill us
tried to flay open our flesh with thin whips   worms came out
of our ass   a beggar asked for help   who are we to believe   for
a second the town opened its gate   we ran inside to a small building   a deer served us   a falcon bid us good day   we no longer
want to be human   it is simple: you need another operation
they're trying to kill you   because you're poor   the poor live
outside the law. our cunts are silver daggers   we shall live in a
new world

Information Sexual Ecstasy
Revolution III

t he moon clashes against the light. you touch me O nympho-
mania!

China. the revolution   a beginning that makes sense   the peas-
ants tortured   without food   turn over   a new life   a (wo)man
wants to control his/her life   I will sacrifice all happiness for the
sake of self-control. I will do anything to maintain my ability to
make decisions. throw the bomb. we plant bombs in the edges
of the rubble   fire escapes below SoHo   we kill everyone! I am
starving   I don't have a phone   I hide the money I've earned
by selling my cunt beneath the stove   in a crack in the wall   I
decide I've earned enough money for four months   decide I'll
stop working   I freak out   A. comes to the door   she's going
to see me with B.   I'm looking at the white sink   I can't control myself   I start crying   I tell A. how I've been getting money
I'm starving   I'm without shelter   I'm scared to walk down the
street   Monsters   she'll be able to find me a part-time shit job
you have to rest   B. doesn't come up   the new world is beginning   a long time elapses   the Cat-Women are meeting   their
purring decides our lives   their huge thighs house our sperm   I
serve a Cat   I lick Her nipples continuously   I mix the cream
of goats   grind corn and wheat   I rub my hair into the inside
of Her legs   I depend for comfort upon every one of Her moods
I stick my tongue into Her black leather lips. I am being con-

trolled. I will plant bombs   I secretly walk along the streets   the
Revolution is one man   the Revolution is the ability to choose
the Revolution is the recognition of   becoming   silver-thighed
nymphomaniacs and whores. beautiful human-animals   I also
am part human   I have given up my humanity   I am one of the
black-winged vulture killers of light.

Kathy Acker (my identity)

all plants and animals burst into flames/light   through the hole
the circle of waters   we walk to the New City at night   flame-
throwers   color bombs   cats fly through your hair   governing
men   the Tao Te Ching   is like governing horses   we are ready
the images are ready   we are ready to move at the first sign of
morning   who do you accept   we accept no one   our criminals stand at the pawnshops   our beggars bite through your
calves   the City bursts into flames   IT explodes   CUNY-Nixon
headquarters explode   at the height   anything   you can do
anything   I'm too scared to ask you to sleep with me   hello
means I'm alive   the government we do over ourselves requires
that we fulfill our regular constant nature then   we be left to
ourselves. this is necessary information   this is to be read slowly
half through dream. the government of the richies   Nixon and
Rockefeller and General Motors   is planting long jellyfish worms
in our bodies   we are asked to be patient   our legs are being
mutilated by giant saws. medical science has advanced. the age
of perfect virtue   this age   will be destroyed by the Teachers'-
Politicians' insistence on the practice of benevolence   righteous-
ness   ceremonies   and music. Power to destruction and chaos
to the half-men hiding beneath the streets the   Cat-Women prey
on dead meat their long legs come down from the sun. O to sleep

between the warm thighs of a Cat-Woman   hair and eyes given vision by her cunt   you mutilated Cat-Woman   your home is in the reaches of the insane moon   you are my partner   you are my partner in the destruction and discovering of paradise. end-of-the-world weather. I'm not scared of being a dyke   huge women   not men   they don't think they're men   they fight with their nipples   they climb up trees to mock at the disappearing cars. I'm not scared anymore   we're not scared anymore   this writing is proof   the revolution needs all our love.

desire.

we desire a revolution in New York   I'm here alone   always alone   Mick Jagger jerks off   I shoulder my pistols   strap on my double chastity belt skunk killer   the cats have disappeared women are hidden under Central Park   in the beds not yet sold breast open to breast   birds wet their fingers   is there a revolution? where's the revolution? someone make love to me   want me to make love to you   the skies break open   BOOM   we know what's going on   RAIN   a sexual-lust-antilobotomy revolution   I desire women therefore am going to be sterilized   brains turn to disease-worms   lips wrenched off by torture-pliers   no pain   pain   I'm happier than I've ever been   the revolution (this) is to be obtained by doing nothing   by passionless and purposeless action   the operation of the heaven and the earth. this is for A.   B.   J.   who I constantly fantasize about   I'm never going to sleep with you. fall asleep in the bath   1½ hours   mind wanders between the moon and its light. about sex.   on Her swing   suspended from the center of the universe   She could lift me   She could treat me as She would a favorite cat playing with me between her foot-long fingers   the exile   She could

throw me into free fall   Her birds with long green tail feathers
red parrots from space   peck at my heart. where does this come
from? we talk to a skull   a Chinese sage with thin wrinkled
hands   we tell him of the happiness of the state after death. this
state. we are crouched in the corners of their closets   we plan
the state's destruction in whatever way possible   the first method
we use   NOW STATED   random choice. flip through the universe without your senses   do not control desire. follow desire
wherever it leads you   take what magic   good and evil   is offered. your hair is pure silver   your cunt is an animal   your thin
face controls my dream.

I move out   onto the streets   tigers and rhinoceroses surround
me   I sniff in the direction of the stars   my killer friends approach   The Man   O.K. last night rape   L. shoots J. in the guts
H.'s mind is slowly being made useless by huge doctors   where
are you going? I won't be able to see you today   L.'s seeing you
        what is real? political action   the negation of evil   the free-
ing of our ability to love   the destruction of the state. chapter
of the day.

new day. Vulture-Killer   I get out of bed I no longer need food
my teeth have holes in them extending to the center of the Universe   I place on foot-long fingers the three magic rings   syphilis
sore on my right ankle   I'm nervous   my muscles are ready to
tense   Mosques rise out of the fertilizer of my beauty   green
eyes   old magic hearts   their spires stick into my cunt through
my fingers I no longer speak sense   pearls ride on the top of
whales   I am I   I am you   *we:*   the new identity if people are
going to remain possible   the hophead who puts his arms around
me by force as if he owns my body is responsible   as I am every

time the doctors purposely kill a poor person   every time the
Teachers destroy   lobotomy   X-ray poison   the brains of a
child   I'm telling you   this is an emergency   we are the emergency   we are not forced to live in pain and to be pain   there is
no one existing outside of us   halls rise   where only nonsense
is spoken   dining rooms of bread and vegetables   cats roam
through the deserted city   rub desire-fur against the skeletons
of men   the Destroyer walks up to me   I'm going to own your
body   BOOM   I'm going to carve up your body with broken
glass   BOOM   I'm telling you who you are I'm a purring cat
flowers in the wild grass   jewels who fold into cloth   I make
the sun rise drench the star in my yellow cunt   I weave hemp to
tie the moon to my sacred waters   the angels who are hermaphroditic fly around my foot-long fingers in which the magic cats
sleep   I am the center of your desire   the Violent Body/Mind
who gives ample food   to each person   shelter with a non-
destroying person   worship of love   the city-sky flames out   the
buildings are fighting against each other   animals graze through
our legs   I make the waters flood   ebb   I make the clouds hide
the Flames.

THE NEW LIFE

Pain Diary

O rose of Silver Angels   Desire that is unending and the Beginning of our loneliness   two legs stronger and wider   the giant beast howls   Light comes from your moon   Freedom! the water of your legs ebbs flows   blood   Fear and Ecstasy we walk side by side   now we know   now we know we walk holding hands   air blows our hair back into whips SWISH   freaks   maniacs   Your schizophrenia   SWISH   Your giant hand covers our eyes   pulls our fingers into long strands of light   Your fingernails scrape the skin off our senses   Your realm is not discussed   there is no language for You   Your cats hide behind our beds   Your spawn   the hermaphroditic angels we can see   lie drunk in our street   You   No-God falling from heaven   Desire outlawed   the Freaks lashed into jails   their brains unhinged   their genitals are destroyed   this is Desire   the new   the new   we push ourselves   we don't know where to go white hair falls around our eyes   blocks our touch   the blackness orange swirls   help   we sink flat   we don't know what we're doing   the Moon sinks down to our eyes   the world is filled   no thing means anything   body despite mescaline   You come down   with tongue touch the center of my cunt   when will we find another formula? propaganda to cling to   repeat zealously   until infinity   You come from the moon   swirl around the moon   at Your pleasure   avoid the light   cause dents in the green flesh with Your fingertips   Your hair flies one inch above our heads   You never rest   You talk to me   in the presence of other people   I am alone   I sit by myself   I cry.

Kathy Acker

*   *   *

change to another person. long black vulture feathers   a thin
horsewhip belt   silver flat shoes (me)   Mick Jagger wears sneakers
relate to you as another person   no   father   mother   no   friend
you fuck three other women per day   no   animals   one the
small replica of the other   mother   daughter   lie beside each
other   tongues lick the tops of heads   fur fluffs out   the Ameri-
cans forbid everything   political actions   P. sucks his cock   constantly asks me to rub his nipples   I'm a white bird   huge curved
beak   I fly above your head   political action leads to all actions
to a world larger than the one in our head we think we're stuck
in relate to somewhere   there. dark sky   I make love with you
four nipples   four sexes   this also will lead to revolution   I go
through the changed world   how changed? my batteries are
down   poetry about poetry   rather stop poetry. no. no   no   NO
NO   change   even shit   I   next to you   you see B. tomorrow
night   do you want to fuck here? I'm going to sleep   Lizzy
knows   she sits next to me   lets me rub her nipples every minute
every piece of matter dies   explodes   every piece of matter is
made. very personal experience   do you know what I'm talking about? there's a world   white birds swoop above the sky   my
material is stolen   junk-writing less than two hours   that's long
a good time to go to sleep   feathers joined to my hands at the
shoulders   flow down my back   the tips of my heels are small
feathers   I never wear makeup   too much anxiety   leather bands
each of my four limbs   I'm walking out your door   I'm disappearing   what do we own? everything   we want to live   quote:
I'm scared of being alone   I'm strong   I talk to you from my
strength otherwise I won't talk   I'm talking about ways of being
relating to other people   you   and you   I'm talking about the
messy way   necessary way   of creating   (political) revolution.

*   *   *

172

change to you and other people. getting along now   slowly   with
my strength   many other people   as I allow them to wound me
I'm not easily destructible   as I allow them their destruction. this
begins this dense   hardly understandable material. through il-
lusions and fantasies who are reality. necessities. you will have
to try to understand. if you want   I will try to   stroke your
breasts and shoulders   breasts that look like mine   to let your
hair sweep over my cunt. you will be scared   (try to) kill me.
you're not gay. I'm not going to walk out the magic door. I'm
not able to put it all together. it'll come out like it comes out. the
birds   who have hidden in your neck   make tiny sounds   SHT
SHT   nonlanguage   you could become a bird   you could try
to support yourself   you could try to destroy. propaganda if it
could be brought out would be the end. desire. I'm forced by
myself   you   the shit society   talk my love for you   not to you
here   to myself.

today people are dancing in the streets.

the worship of beauty   of Angels

we try to find out all motivations   causes of death   the end of
everything. constant diarrhea. can't fuck. charred gray matter
ash   skeletons of men lie in the street especially 81st Street   nowhere to go   Mother   Shit away green disease $ everything
what we want*   utopia   what is happening*   anti-utopia   begin
here   continuous instability   nonpermanence   the procedural
point of view we want to privilege. utopia happening based on
my information   no feelings   (the bridge between today and

) actual knowledge becomes the instrument of the bird flying through black hair   only possible utopia is ʒ love   in the most charred devastated and molten area o. ʌe gray space about 81st Street   stimulate the imagination B. is grumpy mean over the phone   you don't want anything to do with freaks (me)   L. over phone H. over phone   shit 3x   the broken panes are desire   the gays are perfect   will you want? we believe we're able to fly   do anything to go where you want to change to   who you desire   a star   a perfect   the new six points   six tones of music   you fuck with an angel   in mouth in ears   in the space between the lungs   silent center of life   a new self for a new way of living   flexibility is necessary   the city is dead   the city has been destroyed by bombs antimatter evil vibes   the magicians   voodoo signals   poison food   politicians   the rich   Nixon   a series of flying green cocks. I learned today that people are people   not my parents   silver wings sprouted   I gave away my mind   my rings   my invaluable possessions   I destroy the evil   this is a lie   this is a lie   men hide beneath the streets   beneath poison sewers   I want to stop this writing   play chess   you're wrong   I'm living continuously in pain

take my hand   gentle   walk with me through the deserted city the rows of broken neon lights   don't touch me   I've broken through   the skeletons of old men   in the corner is a guy on stage   drag   If I Loved You   a hundred other guys watch him in the dark   on Sundays there are only women   two junkies sell us belts they've stolen   walk out of the shadows   birds fly through the iron rods   the broken dead rot limbs   red   green   yellow no one will show up   here people don't exist anymore   we go past the town   Desert Joe tips his hat   Well   ain't been anyone   here   for   10,000   years   the   Coyote   People   went

underground   Weather-(Wo)men in drag mistakenly committed suicide   once they were rich and affluent   they didn't know
what to do   like you   they thought people were reasonable
common-sense   their shit flew into the sky   angels exploded
leaping through their heads   the angels of light   fur   fur   I'm
taking your hand   where are we going?   don't know   not
going crazy anymore   I've been loving my self   caressing my
self sun worship   you holy exploding flaming sun   how are we
going to eat immediately after the revolution? people can become
snakes   8   the sun becomes plant who become air and animal
who become people who become plant   people desire twine
wind   into themselves   tongues lick inside the fingers heads
come up through gleaming heads   I'm making my movie   L.
and. B. outside the door   wrest control from me   what do they
do? they don't do anything   they own my body   they plant living wasps in the center of my being   destroy my being they stick
long glowing rods into my brains   my cunt   I have to breathe
slowly   my lungs are the center of life   I'm about to explode
panic   we're walking slowly   through the deserted city   bombed-
out   freaked-out city   the realm of evil   we are passing robbers   thieves   gangs of rapists   we are carrying heavy bags of
gold   silver   ride horses with white-and-black fur   our veins
are of gold   we no longer have food   many hours   until morning   we are confused   lost our way   below at the edge of a
wood   we see two lights   a small house   the house of a poor
wood-cutter or a witch   we are protected   we are going toward
the house   the City of Light   we decide   if we are attacked we
should not as we have in the past   flee   now we should try to
love

all foregoing
re: B. not sleeping with me

ABSTRACT ESSAY COLLAGED

WITH DREAMS

Description of the New World

escription of the new world   deer and cats run through
the universe   endless sloping hills   in the haze people
dance   march   walk forward   fists shake   we want   we
want   now   now   silence   dance   you the world I want   don't
know yet   N. is on the radio   gay   joyous   red   yellow   green
orange   we have someone   our love-lust   no   a community
tongue in your   and your warm cunt   fuck   need   want   hun-
ger   crazy   lonely   scared to starve   spend all our time creating for beauty is truth happening history is communist-anarchist
revolution   animals   plants   I rest my head against your knees
my hand moves   gentle   up your leg until you stop me   STOP
HERE   ENTER ALL THE TIME PERIL OF ABSOLUTE JOY
walk on top of the coals   actual guru   through the flames   we
open our mouths   the cat sticks her tongue in   glowing yellow
lights   the sardine gleams   smells   bread dissolves into waves
of lights   bone and hair   the muscle develops   the lights of the
tugboat are electric fish under her hair   she rubs her head between
her paws   eyes are the ever-present pain   eels caress the pits under
her arms   we run down long purple slopes   our robes look like
clouds   at a long table   the house of a former rich man   P.N.   a
thousand green   orange vegetables   sauces made from oil and
grain   salted plums   oil and fertilized eggs   soft white goat cheese
fried lotus root   weeds spring over the bombs of the city   at the
highest heat of the sun   the cats sleep   leopards prowl between
my legs   cold nose sticks into my nostril   no need to leave   come

back   leave   we walk over to purple gold magnetic horses   P.N.
my brother   and my sister   men become women   women men
the actual garments   animals   A. cries out   I feel strongly   I'll
go Tuesday   I don't mind your rich parents   your decadence   the
large garden and stables   I'm sleeping with you sister brother   my
cock is a vine twirling thorn roses through your cunt   call L. to
give information   we announce holy desire

1920   free all prisoners   leave people's minds alone   only our
personal life exists   fish leap through our hair   our limbs tangle
we mutilate each other   take guns slash off our heads   long orange machetes   when we are in bed   make love   the poor   the
starving   the foreign   step across our bodies! throw our walls
flames   gigantic fires   across the night   we have to learn to attack the rich who are the seeds of evil   who start evil out of
covetousness   fear   people will destroy   not return to being
people animals   Ryan   Abzug   McGovern   if the war stops
Vietnam   your shit is piled up a thousand feet high   you have
to change the fiery world   urban guerrilla fighting   no   we're
constantly broke   if we fall down   break an arm   roll over
scream   we might   might not   be accepted by the hospital   we
don't have proper shit credentials   tonight   Dr. X slashes our
arms   at our shoulders   seven times   his mark   don't even
need vaginas   at night   cop comes   get the fuck out   hands
up   hands behind back   slash!   broken arm   who the fuck are
you   who the fuck are you   who the fuck are you   who are
you   how old are you   how old are you   45 minutes pass   go
away   don't bother coming around here   long purple hair   green
hair   arms clasp each other around the burning moon   what
are you going to do   I have to live my own life   learn whatever
I can learn   learn to protect myself   learn to have faith   love

we're insane   we want   we want   we want to decide   will   for
ourselves   welcome   you   the sword is burning   white fire
lights circle wildly around our heads

Gentle   night   walk with me through the yellow pollution   after
you fuck with H. I touch your cunt   still wet   these are facts   I
live with M. and you   desire is insane   insane? after last night
everything is insane   holocaust   we know what we want   community. this is only an essay   female   ass   say   I want   touch
physically love   whoever I want   nymphomaniac rape   I want
to love you   you   you   you   you   when? every 24 hours   the
sun rises   sets   moon rises   sets   plants   make food   animals
and people eat them   when the cats are pleased   their eyes close
black slits against the sun   their orange ears come forward into
our hands   physical   body   desire   is holy   hollering   screaming   I'm rubbing my scarred face against your knees   my tongue
is flickering back   forth   fast   your small nipples   I come   we
come   the oceans are formed   every   act is political and sexual
you can't live in a nonsexual community   impossible   consider
the thousand sexual desires   lust for a child and a dying bird
you're telling me what to think? I'm not political   you want to
use my work   me   as much as possible   cat goes crazy   her
paws around pink black star   she bites   chews   rolls on the bed
tail rushes up   swings from a flaming star   if we could do what
we wanted   if we could   we're going insane   fearful   out of
control   decision   antirevolutionary-anti-Marxist contradictions
we pretend we're someone else   we can't handle (disguise) ourselves   silver touch   touch   lie on L.'s belly   I am the goddess
I control   we need to control   be controlled   we have it planned
out we   now k-now   now k-now

*   *   *

6/17/72   silver hair   snow falls inside the eye   you   tree and
birch and plant   be with us   now   we have become insane   we
have thrown ourselves into the outer world   essay on our madness

we make new form   new   everything   we are now   making   sing
sing   the cats   the slinking   touch   body   crazy   glowing alone
space   lights   thousands of lights   everything act is here   is happening   is in touch   touching at now   instant   a narration   thousands of narrations   political   sexual   sensual   holy   velvets
tapestries about Buddhas   gurus   monks   bent in mudras   for
four thousand years   forty thousand years ago   tigers fucked
small men   swamps preserved them   the huge cats sat on the stone
walls   ivy grows out of our cunts   ground! ground! American red
form   distinguish from this evil America this   America   we are
destroying   in the process of   annihilate   yes   I can stay alive
economically through shit-work   and write   learn   the shit-work
logic   outgrowth-base of the evil rich   write   write-ing   is   doing
destruction   touching   fucking   you   all of you   keeping   lust
for you   all future glorious lovers   not now known   I lonely
praise   Gertrude Stein   Walt Whitman   Allen Ginsberg   the
women of you   America   apocalypse   visions   who fly to the
raging beams   moon   one revolution every 1/3 second   faster
than any dynamite thought   you who are licking   drinking out
of the acid cunt of the moon   legs spread beyond the supposed
sphere of the universe   twirled in ivy vines

I am writing about every thing-being   I am can do every thing-
being   decide   decide   incredible horny   desirous   about to
no   leave my body   be only body   fly upward past the stories
women sit at various floors   green trees shoot out of the stone

do what I want   you future-fuck-lovers-women-men   with the
mile-long scissors   I cut off my silver hair.

specific   gold   information   B.   the government does
not want the people to learn.

VIOLET WOMEN

Narration of the New World

flowers: dandelions   large   small carnations   pussy willows
milk buds   roses   tulips   lilies of the valley   daisies   daffodils
hyacinths   arise. cats become people   roam the countries
sniff nose   stare at running silver. this is the new world. first: fear
desire. we are more scared than we have to be. mind blown by
THE GREAT DICTATOR. wish you were here. this is the new
world   green cats   lions   ten-feet-long whiskers frighten away
the Evil Ones   you know   the black pit   the nights   the earth
is sufficient   started growing   we know nothing   silver ears
grow through the tops of our heads   silver mouths grow through
our mouths   you come through the door   I sit on your legs   I
kiss your mouth   you take us far   you take us into the first cores
of the outer suns   the Violet Women are now animals   cats   glowing   burning panthers prowl on the tops of your bodies   there
is nothing you can do   there is nothing you can do   we are All-
sex   we fly fire   blue fire is over your bodies   you lie in bed
scared always   touch   you kill your children   you come   you
know the world is your eyes   your lips   inch of your outer and
inner bodies   we are alone   not (constantly) scared of each other
black orange gray white skies sail through our minds through love
comes everything   every opening   the curtains   a hand reaches
up   the mother shows meat   red drip   human leg   the Evil One
grabs it   the mother turns away   slitted blue eyes   smile   later
they take the killed child up the stones   roll his body in garbage
the tooth is magic   the milk of the donkey is magic   in the flames

the burning of my desire that is never satisfied   this is the new
world   poets bums criminals drunks want   die for love   even
the worship of death   this is always what is happening   angels
rise in our heart

what is this a narration of? H. is the enemy   she ruins my work
by making me work with M.   M. is good now she doesn't like
M.'s work   she wants M. to show her work in my show because
it will be good for M.'s head. H. is supposed to like me. I'm split-
ting apart   I'm walking through solid black murk   I'm not able
to see anyone   because I have deserted her   H. tells other people
I'm not beautiful   my breasts   droopy   ugly. I'm a child   I
don't know how to act   I hurt other people's feelings. H. wants
to destroy me. I won't be able to reclaim my work   I've committed myself to M. I've forever ruined this first chance to show
my work in New York   H. is my friend   I mustn't in any way
hurt her   I must touch her black head if she wants me to   I'm
her protector   she can slowly slice through my lips with a sharpened razor   I never hurt   different color reds   the room   the
room   communist   what the hell does nonpolitical work have
to do with mine? this is the way we keep in touch   each other
and ourselves   hold hands   we swirl through the black court-
yard   white leaves   we levitate   kiss   where is this going to get
us? it doesn't matter   eyes like a deer's   belly   touch   belly   we
end   standing over a grave   Theosophilis and Elizabeth Brxxx
is a person lying under where we're standing   yes   laughs   don't
worry   every thing-being is political   you laugh   these are my
friends: X   scratch   no   I can live better alone   close   no
closer   J. and M. show up   the forest   their eyes come up through
the branches   this is beginning a narration   second narration
the existence of enemies and friends   the striving toward freedom
includes animal   plants   people   this is a beginning   because

I saw N. decided to go to the dance   in which the leaves bow   to each other and leave   the dandelions decide to sleep   the cats are quiet   the gay women kiss   become (communist) men.

H. is dead. a huge bird flies down   slices off her head. her hands become long jelly-snakes. she wants to be a commercial success she wants a home before she dies   buy   one   three   over the bodies of dead wo-men   now starting   the children cry   shriek hold   me   hold   me   we no   they become everything   they do anything you want   they are repeating you   word   for word. the children underneath the ground   in the mountains   a foot beneath the waters of the canyons   where live the dwarves green giants cry out   filled up by rich white-masked cigars   with millions of milligrams of speed and belladonna   shot by force into their broken arms   they now sit on the branches of the forest   HOOT   HOOT   the children   killed by us and by them-selves   wombs are now mounds of cow manure   can do any-thing   they live below the ancient mosques   they plan guerrilla attacks on the rich spires of the city   the holy dogs who fucked M.   raised for a thousand years by Persian princes   who leap straight in the air on the back of boars   WOOF   we like them destroy   the dogs   walk through the hidden country the dirt lanes under the concrete streets   the leaves hidden in the green puss   what is this? this is silver propaganda   propaganda against those who are enemies against those who are hurting us   infil-trate our skin and blood   for ideals   stick slow   tortuous poi-sons in our guts. I have silver hair and strong thighs   I play baseball walk like a cowboy   down the deserted halls   the Empire State Building crumbles   beautiful! educational centers smother them-selves   we advocate all destruction   without loss of life   nowhere necessary   beautiful! all lives are chaos   pits on the green swirling moon   this is information   part of propaganda   worship of all people

Personal Life

to be female wo-man is alone constantly on guard as independent as possible always prepared to be without shelter possibilities of talk a secret language daily language to be various ways and talk various ways are strong weapons live a life which is secret to nonwomen who live otherwise the only way in which to be women is to act in certain ways to think in certain ways sexual gender no longer exists to know you have to be strong at every moment to be able to talk to X each other without having to puzzle what to say without having to plan how to control X you are always your own home your lover the child the mother and the father it is necessary for the survival of earth perhaps universe life that more all humans become decide women effeminacy fem twine we must be mentally masturbatory in the mountains the caves a foot below the waters of the canyons the cockroach cities you must act out there is no more choice I am going to die whatever I do I We are related to the huge strong-limbed giants in the moon. the ants march by kill H. they live in the holes the green sores of the street pus drools out of their mouths they do not die disappear like yellow dust. Sunday. H. calls I don't want her I fly away. it is necessary decide you are female. Women ↔ then ↔ women. men are humans who are bred trained they can do anything they are almighty they must not be concerned with daily life. their essence is rape. their desire is murder. they are forced to destroy. sexual gender not exist. you do what you want.

write about as you live. the dance begins. the cats appear   prowl
through the gardens   the clocks move back. dwarves   giants
come out of the caves   giant dildos strapped to their thighs. you
are the child of the princess   your hair is burnt away by a star.

this is promise   Earth Mother   Mother of Skies   her who is
orange   Silver   hair out of her eyes   her gods messengers are the
cats   promise   Her   my suffering will not disappear   I work
through suffering   the orange cat is part of the earth   the orange
blanket in the morning   before the morning   is Her   rising now
in communist glory   this is Her   announce   the things as they
exist   the actions   the relations   Violet Women will take over
the earth   by being the earth-sky   they enter into circumstances
they are bitchy as all hell   New York   a yellow ball comes down
top of our heads   our faces change   noses elongate   last night   I
pray   to the Mother   I give my Silver self to her   morning: now:
I want to make love to one of the M. twins in my school   she wants
to make love to me   Silver eyes enter into long blonde hair   she
is thinner   the bones in face stick out.   I call E. and B.   I'm a
mobster   I take their money   I inject syphilis into the center of
the earth. they return love. all   happening   is praise to Her   of
the orange hair. B. killed   then slept with X.   I no longer listen
this is a story   the Violet Women   hand   through sky   touches
hand   through water   touches third hand   until the beginning
interwoven   chariots ride through the sharp green spears   orange
blue fish in the glades   star-alligators   who are the Violet Women
they are the deliverers   I am not I   the Violet Women are a long
work as slowly as I learn to come   together fight   I am strong
beginning   give self to the Mother   syphilis reigns in my body   eyes
rise through the mosques   this   is the story and it will take a long
time   it will never be ending   start   I wake up   I rise out of bed
I let in the cats   I wake up   I rise   up   orange   fur   black

brown   orange   fur   fur rubs against my feet   hours pass   I call
B.   I can't play baseball   no help   work   no   get off phone   I'm
moving   this depends on my living   get sense through   I dedicate my heart   mind   we all of us   want   a cat jumps through
the glades   one paw   second paw   third paw   one paw   belly
all clawed   glaze in eyes   kiss   kiss   kiss   kiss   kiss   kiss   curtains   blows away breeze   comes up tonight   our goal   the bum
and criminal are our midnight to come

B.   bum and arch-criminal   love.

spires   now we have murdered $ whirl through purple clouds
the heads of angels   space   three kinds of space   yellow space
blue space   velvet space   space inside and outside   the head   are
animals   now   we live alone   free   the cats of the universe have
two tails   one   black and white checks   curls over the head   into
infinity   the second tail   the center of the head   around the back
feet   down the gold of the ass. we reach out to the moon   curl
round strange purple lichen thongs   exploding new satellites who
bum around the universe   to our wrists   tails wind around our
wrists   our thin fingers   leather bands   we raise our hands
through air   clench fists   huge jewels only   the poor possess   our
breasts licked hard by strings of berries and diamonds   our birth-
stone   desire each other   our cunts wrap into the glory of other
worlds   do whatever you want   we do whatever we want   do
whatever you want   we do whatever we want   we are now roam-
ing through the states of the universe   this is a map for future
journeys   love   a white ball rolls in the center of the void   who
decides? the female dogs of the Persian king   leap straight in the
air   come down on the backs of wild boars   they trot the streets
like horses   at the fair   anchovies wrapped around capers   red

plums peaches   grapes for champagne   strawberries   raspberries
blackberries   blueberries   huge leaves   apples   bananas   dried
spices   salt cod   squashes a mile long   Chinese string beans   pup-
pet shows for the horses   cats prowl in the streets above the booths
they roll in our hair   gardens contain gold leaves   gold branches
an arm lifts out of each well   insects become people   people become horses   horses appear out of the mists   rays   shoot from
our fingers   we love for a thousand years

the Violet Women   you and I   raise our fists   we suck off Nixon
McGovern   Nixon and McGovern embrace   they are buggering
McGovern wins   he sticks thin long white cock into Nixon's
asshole   Nixon dosen't wipe his ass when he shits   McGovern
and Eagleton put hands on each other's waists   they fall in love!
they all raise hands   they proclaim anarchy   they vow to give the
government back to the people. what happens? the Violet Women
know   the Violet Women are all-powerful and have no power over
anyone else   they take care of themselves   they are not teachers-
analysts-doctors of all kinds-lawyers   their arm hair curls around
their ankles   gold cunt hair   runs up their legs   grows out of fer-
tile star navels   psychoanalysis? no. government? no. family? no.
the Violet Women keep to themselves   DO NOT APPROACH
beware   it takes days to trust someone enough to talk   to her
admit we know   we love   fire causes love   spread legs cause love
terror repressed desire   subterranean war   cause   undying love
the Violet Women hide in large caves   huge muscles grow on their
legs   they rub against the yellow mud   in times of starvation   they
eat their protein-shit   a sickness? they accept whatever they feel
as exactly they feel   they will never lose their virginity   they will
fuck three million men   every golden hour   they pat mud in their
hair   huge turretted castles   no guards   moats in which swim
thousands of different fish   the children fly through the air   they

grunt   have three separate languages they use for different intensi-
ties of feelings   they stamp feet   touch hands   and free skin   for
holy music   in times terror   they hide   or they change identities
they become each other   they don't have to have identity   they
can remain functioning   self   they watch the sky change color
dawn   herds of pigs pass by   they hide gallons of alcohol in their
breasts.

THE PURPOSE
GENTLENESS LOVE INTO THE REVOLUTION   NOT OC-
CURRING IN POLITICS   LOVE B.   WHEN THE NARRA-
TIVE IS OVER   SOMETHING   NEW. ENVY. JOY. DO NOT
KILL   LEARN. THIS IS OUTER SPACE MESSAGE   WANDER-
ING THE COSMOS. FOOTLOOSE CAT-SKUNKS THOUGHTS
ARE GUINEA PIGS   HOP-BRAIN   LONG HAIR   BLACK
BROWNS   SILVER   ALL OUTER SPACE MESSAGES   WE
ARE LEGALLY FREAKED   WE MUST COMMUNICATE
SUCK CUNT SUCK CUNT   NIPPLE FIGHT   YES WE ARE
CONCERNED WITH CHANGE WORLD   I SHIT IN MY
PANTS   CONSTANT   STREAM   OF   GODDESS   WORDS
LIGHT EXISTS IN A THOUSAND COLORS   A THOUSAND
DIVISIONS OF EACH ARBITRARY COLOR   THOUSAND
DIVISIONS OF EACH DIVISION . . . SUCK CUNT   YOUR
RELATION TO ME IS   YOUR RELATION IN THE DREAM
MY FACE IS WRAPPED IN GOLDEN CLOTH   A CASKET
AND A RING GIVE ME WHAT I NEED   THREE KEGS OF
ALE   TEN LOAVES OF BREAD   ONE FISH   SOME TEA
I'M FLYING OVER NEW YORK   FIVE IRON BARS
DOMINO SUGAR TRUCK PASSES   WOMEN AND MEN
ALL POETS BECOME OTHER POETS   SAY THE SAME
LINES   ST. MARK'S CHURCH IS A REVOLUTIONARY
CRUISE-JOINT   LACK OF BOOZE   TOO MUCH DOPE
NOT ENOUGH DOPE   NO X TO PUT ARMS AROUND

MY BODY   EYES ↔ EYES   BELLY ↔ BELLY   BREASTS ↔ BREASTS   DO I SUFFER   DO WE SUFFER   YOU SEE PSYCHIATRIST-CREEP EVERY DAY   DO YOU ALLEVI- ATE SUFFERING   DO YOU HAVE ENOUGH FOOD   DO WE HAVE ENOUGH FOOD CONDITIONS BEFORE THE REVOLUTION WILL BE THE CONDITIONS AFTER THE REVOLUTION   WHO WANTS SOMEONE TO TELL HER WHAT TO DO   WHO WANTS TO LEND HER BODY TO THE POLICE FORCE   THE BURNING PUBLIC LIBRARY B. IS A REVOLUTIONARY BODY   WE ARE GOLD TONGUES GOLD HANDS   OUTER SPACE   DELIGHTS   WE GIVE JOY WE GIVE MISERY   WE GIVE PLEASURE   WE GIVE IMMORTALITY-HEALTH   WE ARE ENDLESS MIND-BODY PLEASURE ORGA (NI) SM

OUTER SPACE MESSAGES

TOTAL CHAOS!

WE CHOOSE WORK   FOR LONELINESS   LACK
OF HUMANS   LOVE US   FEAR   FOOD AND
SHELTER   FEAR   THE STAR FLOATS IN SPACE
SKY   WE ARE STRONG AND WOMEN   DESIRE   COLD
SHELTER   0° TO 30°F. WE LEAP ACROSS THE HORNS OF
BULLS   THE ICICLES OF SEVEN COLORS   VISION IS FIRST
EXPERIMENTS-JOURNEYS WE SEE   WE FLY   MOUN-
TAINS   HAIR GROWS OUT OF OUR UPPER LEGS   WE
LEARN ABOUT EVERYTHING! WE KNOW   WHICH STAR
MOVES AROUND WHICH STAR   INTO THE MOUTH
OF THE SACRED BEAR   PLANNED NET EXPLODES   TOO
MANY BOMBS   TOO MANY HUMANS   ARE WE HUMAN?
YOU SLEEP WITH WHOM YOU WANT   ALL X'S INCLUDE
NIXON-CREEP   WANT YOU   YOU NEVER MAKE BED
UNBELIEVABLE LACK OF STRUCTURE   CHAOS   IN LIFE-
LIVING   HOW BEAUTIFUL! HURRY UP   HURRY UP
NIXON'S GOING TO BLOW UP SOUTH AMERICA   TOO
MUCH SAUERKRAUT   MCGOVERN DOESN'T DO ANY-
THING   MR. ABBIE HOPMAN   YOU ALSO BEAUTIFUL   I
FUCK YOU   ANYTIME   NEITHER $ NOR TIME EXISTS
WHERE ARE WE GOING   ROSES   PEACHES   BLUE EYES
A MILLION SILVER BEDS   I GIVE PRESENTS   PRESENTS
DO NOT EXIST   REVOLUTIONS DO NOT EXIST BUT
ANARCHY   ANARCHY   WILL   BE   EVER   PRESENT
THROUGH ALL FUTURE LIVING-LIFE

THE SKY IS PURPLE BLUE. MY LEGS ARE WIND.
WATER POURS FROM MY GOLD CUNT TO THE FLOOR.
WE-TOGETHER ARE EQUI-LIBRIUM   WE STUDY   THE
DISTANT PLANETS   THE NATURE OF LIVING ORGAN-
ISMS   THE RELATIONS BETWEEN MATTER   ENERGY
TIME   THE NATURES OF MATTER   ENERGY   TIME
THE RELATIONS   THIS UNIVERSAL NO LEDGE EXIS-
TENCE   AND OUR BEING SOCIAL RELATIONS. WE BE
MOUNTAINS   MOUNTAINS RUN   HOW   A COW RUNS
INTO THE OCEAN   NOW WE   GO   FROM HERE   ANAR-
CHY IS NECESSARY   DELIGHT   JOY   PLEASURE   OPEN
DAY   FREE   DOING   UNINTERRUPTED   GAYETY.

THE VIOLET WOMEN   WE   ARE   BEAUTY   STRENGTH
SEX   DEVOUR   LET BE   INTELLIGENCE OF THE STARS
WISDOM   COOL   MILLIONS OF ORGASMS   ENOUGH
TO   END ANYONE ELSE'S LIFE. HIGH   ON A ROCK   WE
SIT   WINGS SPREAD OVER ONE THOUSAND YEARS
DOODY-FARM HOUSES   BLACK DOGS YELP   TOUCH
THE EDGES OF FINGERS   EYE OF CHRIST LOOKS INTO
EYE   HUGE WHITE FEATHERS ACROSS THE NONHU-
MAN SNOW   IN THE HALL   NO LIGHT   A RED CIRCLE
BODIES OF BEAUTIFUL ANIMALS LINE THE CORNERS   A
HUGE BICYCLE   CHINA! WE SIT   WAIT   STEAL TWO
BOTTLES OF LOWENBRAU   YOUR LEGS ARE SHAVED   I
TOUCH YOUR ANKLE   LIGHTNING FLASHES   WE ARE
WAITING FOR THE WORLD TO BEGIN   WE SLOWLY
FORGE OUR STRENGTH   OUR DOUBLE SEX   A THOU-
SAND GIGANTIC BIRDS   BURST OUT OF THE SPHERE
RAYS OF COLOR   RED   BLUE   PURPLE   BIRDS ZOOM
AROUND IN SPACE   THE GREEN EYES OF CATS   WITH
LEGS SPREAD   HANDS ON THE BOTTLES OF BEER   LOOK

AROUND! INCREDIBLE TRAIN SCHEDULES   IN PEKING
THE STREETS ARE 200 FEET WIDE   THE GARDENS   ARISE
FUCHSIAS   DWARF TREES   TULIPS   CHERRIES   THE
BIRDS REST HERE   A MOMENT   WAY TO THE NORTH
THE PEOPLE HAVE ENOUGH AND NO MORE   HERE
THE PEOPLE HAVE NOTHING   WE HAVE NOTHING
AMERICA   DOESN'T THAT HAVE TO DO WITH EVERY-
THING? WE HAVE NO GRAIN   I FIND GRAIN   I PROPOSI-
TION THE GRAIN   GRAIN COMING   OUT OF THE
MOTHER   WE WEAR ONLY SCARVES AROUND OUR
NECKS   WE SIT ON TOP OF THE BONES OF TIGERS
TIGERS ENTWINED WITH THE GREEN MONSTERS THEY
FOUGHT BEFORE ANY PEOPLE EXISTED   100-FEET-
LONG BIRDS SWOOPED DOWN   BITE   THE BACKS OF
THEIR NECKS THEY PUT ARMS AROUND EACH
OTHER'S NECKS   20-FOOT CATS   THEY WATCH EACH
OTHER   TIME   TAIL   SWISH   TAIL   SWISH   FUR FLIES
OUT TO THE EDGES OF THE UNIVERSE   THE EARTH
IS FLAT   WE FALL OFF THE EDGE   GOLD SPLENDOR
WHERE GOLD IS CONSTANT   NO MARK OF IMPERIAL-
ISM   GHOSTS SAY THEY OWN ME   BODY*HEART*
MIND   ESCAPE BURNING   HEART-SUN   LONG FIRE ES-
CAPE   DESCEND INTO THE EARTH   EAT THE REST OF
MY HEART